THE
SILVER HILLS BOARDING HOUSE

THE SILVER HILLS BOARDING HOUSE

**Also by #1 *New York Times* bestselling author
Linda Lael Miller**

Painted Pony Creek
Where the Creek Bends
Christmas at Painted Pony Creek
Country Born
Country Proud
Country Strong

The Carsons of Mustang Creek
A Snow Country Christmas
Forever a Hero
Always a Cowboy
Once a Rancher

The Brides of Bliss County
Christmas in Mustang Creek
The Marriage Season
The Marriage Charm
The Marriage Pact

The Parable Series
Big Sky Secrets
Big Sky Wedding
Big Sky Summer
Big Sky River
Big Sky Mountain

McKettricks of Texas
An Outlaw's Christmas
A Lawman's Christmas
McKettricks of Texas: Austin
McKettricks of Texas: Garrett
McKettricks of Texas: Tate

The Creed Cowboys
The Creed Legacy
Creed's Honor
A Creed in Stone Creek

Stone Creek
The Bridegroom
The Rustler
A Wanted Man
The Man from Stone Creek

The McKettricks
A McKettrick Christmas
McKettrick's Heart
McKettrick's Pride
McKettrick's Luck
McKettrick's Choice

Mojo Sheepshanks
Arizona Heat (originally published as *Deadly Deceptions*)
Arizona Wild (originally published as *Deadly Gamble*)

The Montana Creeds
A Creed Country Christmas
Montana Creeds: Tyler
Montana Creeds: Dylan
Montana Creeds: Logan

THE SILVER HILLS BOARDING HOUSE

Linda Lael Miller

CANARY STREET PRESS

CANARY
STREET
PRESS™

ISBN-13: 978-1-335-42476-1

The Silver Hills Boarding House

Copyright © 2025 by Hometown Girl Makes Good, Inc.

All rights reserved. No part of this book may be used or reproduced in any manner whatsoever without written permission.

Without limiting the exclusive rights of any author, contributor or the publisher of this publication, any unauthorized use of this publication to train generative artificial intelligence (AI) technologies is expressly prohibited. Harlequin also exercises their rights under Article 4(3) of the Digital Single Market Directive 2019/790 and expressly reserve this publication from the text and data mining exception.

This is a work of fiction. Names, characters, places, and incidents are either the product of the author's imagination or are used fictitiously. Any resemblance to actual persons, living or dead, businesses, companies, events or locales is entirely coincidental.

TM is a trademark of Harlequin Enterprises ULC.

Canary Street Press
22 Adelaide St. West, 41st Floor
Toronto, Ontario M5H 4E3,
Canada
CanaryStPress.com

HarperCollins Publishers
Macken House, 39/40 Mayor Street Upper,
Dublin 1, D01 C9W8, Ireland
www.HarperCollins.com

Printed in U.S.A.

For Audrey Dean, angel of finance, with deep gratitude.

ONE

September 1921
Silver Hills, Montana

The dry dirt of Main Street roiled and soared around Elizabeth "Lizbet" Fontaine as she stepped down from the jitney, the last to exit, after her stepfather, his new wife and the children, Frankie and Jubal, her half sister and brother.

She ached all over from the crowding and the constant jolting and jostling of the open-sided conveyance as it rattled, huffed and popped over cattle trails and a few rocky, crooked passages generously called roads. She was coated in grit, not just on the outside, but inside her mouth, her nostrils and her ears, too.

Her pale copper hair, which she regarded as her best feature, was grimy, and here she'd washed it so carefully just that morning, at the hotel in Kalispell. Given it precisely one hundred strokes with her natural bristle brush, too, once it had had a little time to dry.

Now it felt like straw, and her scalp itched.

Behind her, the jitney emitted a sound so reminiscent of a gunshot that Lizbet jumped, placed one tremulous hand to the base of her throat.

Purposefully, she squared her shoulders and lifted her chin.

In that moment, though, she would have given everything she had, which admittedly wasn't a great deal, for a long soak in a bathtub full of clean, hot water, followed by a change of clothes and a good meal.

Her stepfather, William Keller, beckoned to her to join him and Marietta, his bride of six months, on the broad board sidewalk in front of Happy Jack's General Store.

Marietta, standing close beside her doting husband, linked a possessive arm with his. She was a stunning creature, Marietta was, an erstwhile stage actress who hoped to become a film star once she and William reached their final destination: Hollywood, California.

Marietta's ice-blue eyes narrowed as Lizbet dutifully complied with her stepfather's summons, and her dark, fashionably short hair gleamed in the afternoon sunshine.

There was no love lost between the two women, though Lizbet tried to keep the peace for the sake of the children.

Her sister, Frances, known as Frankie, was only eight years old, and Jubal, their brother, just five.

Both of them were still reeling from the sudden loss of their mother, and Lizbet's, barely a year before, and neither of them had taken to Marietta, who made no effort whatsoever to comfort either little one, let alone mother them.

Frankie and Jubal were, in fact, the only reason Lizbet had agreed to leave her position as a teacher at a private girls' school back home in St. Louis and set out for the raucous, ill-behaved West.

At twenty-two, Lizbet was already considered a spinster, although that had never troubled her much. She'd loved her job, and she'd had her share of suitors—none of whom met her standards, alas, since she was in no hurry to tie herself down.

In California, she had long since decided, she would find another position—her references were impeccable—and establish a modest but respectable home for herself, Frankie and Jubal.

As Lizbet moved toward her waiting stepfather, Frankie and Jubal followed close on the heels of her scuffed shoes, Jubal actually catching hold of her skirt.

Neither child liked to let Lizbet out of their sight, at least not since their mother's sudden death from pneumonia.

She felt a pang of sorrow and took that small, grubby hand firmly into her own. Squeezed once, to let the boy know she wasn't going to leave him.

He was depending on her, and so was Frankie. Desperately so.

"Elizabeth," her stepfather said, as another man approached. He was dressed much the way William was, although his tailor-made trousers, waistcoat and linen shirt were clean. "There is someone I want you to meet. He's an old friend of mine."

Marietta folded her arms across her shapely chest and smirked a little.

"This is Mr. Henry Middlebrook," William said buoyantly, his smile white and wide in his dusty face, as though he were introducing Lizbet to the President himself. "Henry, my stepdaughter, Miss Elizabeth Fontaine."

Something inside Lizbet shrank back as she took in Mr. Middlebrook, who was, it seemed, a friend or business associate of William's. He was portly, bewhiskered and, she saw as he swept off his pristine top hat and bowed slightly, quite nearly bald.

His tiny brown eyes swept over Lizbet's person at outrageous leisure, and she suppressed a shudder. His smile made her cringe, though she managed not to show it.

Actually, if it hadn't been for Frankie and Jubal, and the sad fact that she had nowhere to go, Lizbet would have turned on her heel and walked—perhaps run—away. In that exact moment.

Alas, for the time being, she was decidedly stuck.

"You are certainly a lovely sight to see, Miss Elizabeth," remarked Mr. Middlebrook, his tone oily-smooth. "May I call you Elizabeth?"

Lizbet hesitated.

Out of the corner of her eye, she saw that Marietta's mocking smile was still in place, and she felt a sudden and fierce need to slap the woman square across that rouged and powdered face with all the strength she had.

"Of course you may," William interjected, his voice jovial.

No, Lizbet thought. *No, Mr. Middlebrook. You may not call me by my given name.*

But she said nothing.

Frankie and Jubal were her mother's children, yes, but they were William's flesh and blood as well, and legally he had all the say-so where they were concerned. He paid them little mind, most of the time, being consumed by Marietta and his business holdings, but there was some kind of scheme brewing between him and his elderly cohort, and Lizbet couldn't afford to cross him.

Not just yet, anyway.

At that moment, a surrey came around the next bend in the road, followed by a rustic wagon pulled by mules, and stopped alongside the still-sputtering jitney. The wagon halted, too, though at a small distance.

The fancy rig was new, still smelling of leather and oil, drawn by two immaculately groomed horses, both black as coal.

Lizbet was reminded of a hearse, and a chill trickled down her spine like droplets of water from a melting icicle.

Had this man come with a surrey and a buckboard, simply to squire the little party to the town's one hotel? No. Something was definitely amiss.

"May I?" Mr. Middlebrook asked, his tone sleazy somehow, like the predatory expression on his face as he offered his arm to Lizbet.

She stiffened, ready to dig in her heels.

The old man didn't wait for an answer; he took Lizbet firmly by the elbow and steered her forcibly toward the waiting surrey.

"Now see here," she protested, stumbling a little, shocked and indignant.

He ignored her.

Jubal clung to Lizbet's hand, and now Frankie was clutching at her skirt.

"Sir," Lizbet snapped, stung by the man's audacity. "Kindly remove your hand from my arm!" She felt the heat of primal fury climb her grimy neck and throb in her cheeks.

Beneath his patchy white beard, Mr. Middlebrook's slack jaw tightened visibly, though his smile remained, fixed and devoid of all good humor.

The world seemed to fall silent and still around Lizbet then, around all of them, as if they were figures in a photograph or a painting, not living, breathing people.

It was William who broke the spell; he gave a boisterous laugh, as though they were all players in a lively comedy. "Don't be difficult, Elizabeth," he wheedled, pretending to fondness, though she recognized the grim undercurrent coursing beneath his sunny words and countenance. "Mr. Middlebrook is our host, and he's a very important man."

Lizbet jerked her arm free of Henry Middlebrook's too-familiar grip, stepped back and pulled the children against her sides, holding them tightly.

It was at that moment that another voice interjected, "Leave the lady alone, Henry. She's made her preferences clear, after all."

Lizbet, her breath so fast and so shallow she feared she might actually swoon, turned her head and saw a tall, solemnly handsome man standing a few feet away.

He carried a bulging burlap bag over one broad shoulder, and very briefly, despite his decisive manner, Lizbet glimpsed an immeasurable sorrow behind his gray eyes.

His hair was dark, a little too long, but clean, and his hands looked strong. His clothes were typical of a farmer: dungarees and a frayed cotton shirt.

He walked with a slight limp, an indication that he might have served in the Great War. Perhaps that accounted for the flash of sadness she'd seen a moment before.

Lizbet stifled a ridiculous urge to run to this stranger and fling herself into his arms.

"I don't recall asking for your opinion, Gabe," Mr. Middlebrook said in an easy drawl that didn't match the barely bridled fury he exuded, along with the smells of heavy cologne, whiskey and sweat. "Why don't you just run along on home, back to that little farm of yours, and tend to your own business?"

Gabe flung the bag, which probably contained feed,

into the bed of an already-loaded buckboard Lizbet had failed to notice before.

Having done that, he placed his hands on his hips, regarded Mr. Middlebrook skeptically and replied, "When a man tries to take a woman someplace she doesn't want to go, it's my business, all right."

His gaze linked with Lizbet's, asking a silent question.

"There really is no cause for concern—er—Gabe," William butted in. "Henry here is a family friend, and he's merely trying to be courteous. I'm afraid Lizbet—Elizabeth—is somewhat overwrought from the long, difficult journey we've just made."

"I'll need to hear that from Miss Elizabeth, Mister," Gabe answered. "That's she's all right with getting into that surrey, I mean."

Lizbet felt rooted to the ground, hard beneath her sore feet, which had swollen inside her plain and practical shoes.

She looked at the children, then at this man called Gabe. Was he named for Gabriel, the archangel? It was a foolish and fanciful thing to wonder, but in that moment, it seemed fitting if he was.

"Are we going to the hotel?" Lizbet inquired of her stepfather, surprised by the calmness in her own voice, because inside, she was anything but calm.

William sighed a long-suffering sigh.

Marietta glared. Tapped one expensively shod foot.

Mr. Middlebrook said nothing; he merely glowered at Gabe.

Finally, after a short, charged silence, William spoke again, addressing Lizbet. "We're having dinner at Henry's home," he said carefully. Evenly. "After that, we'll make our way to the Statehood Hotel, where we have reservations."

Lizbet was tired, and a lot of the fight had gone out of her. She needed food and rest before she dealt with this unexpected situation.

Not once had her stepfather mentioned Mr. Middlebrook, let alone relayed plans to dine with the man.

She looked at Gabe, feeling as slack as an understuffed scarecrow after a hard rain, and replied bleakly. "I think we'll be fine, Mr.—"

"Whitfield," he replied. "Gabe Whitfield."

"Mr. Whitfield, then," Lizbet said, as though some important matter had been settled. "Thank you kindly for your concern."

Gabe Whitfield's fine mouth moved slightly, as though he wanted to smile but wasn't quite able to do it, and he nodded. "Anytime," he said.

Then, to Lizbet's surprise—and vague relief—he nodded toward a two-story white clapboard house on the other side of the road.

Lizbet hadn't noticed that before, either.

Thus, she hadn't seen the tiny black woman sitting on the porch in a rocking chair. She was huddled in the folds of a bulky shawl, despite the warmth of the day, and even from that distance, Lizbet could see that she was watching the scene unfolding in front of the general store with dour interest.

"You need a place to run to," Gabe Whitfield went on, "you just head for Mrs. Ornetta Parkin's boarding house right over there—that's her, in the rocking chair. She's a fine woman, and she'll take you in—" Here, he paused and allowed his steady gaze to drift back to Mr. Middlebrook's rapidly reddening face. "And she'll see that you're safe. The children too, of course. If the need arises, send for me and I'll do whatever I can to help."

Afraid to look at her stepfather, or Mr. Middlebrook, who had backed off, although she could almost feel him simmering like a full kettle fixing to blow off its lid, Lizbet stored up the information she'd just been given.

"Thank you," she said moderately, moments later, tempted to take Frankie's and Jubal's hands and march right over to throw herself and the children on Ornetta Parkin's mercy. "I'll keep that in mind."

Gabe nodded, turned and walked away. Climbed into the seat of his buckboard, released the brake lever with a motion of one foot and brought down the reins.

Too soon, he'd rounded a corner and vanished.

"Is he a cowboy?" Jubal asked, with a note of admiration in his voice. He still hung on to Lizbet's hand with a grip that was almost painful, but his gaze had followed Gabe Whitfield and his wagon out of sight.

"I don't know," Lizbet murmured in reply, struck by the wistful note the words carried. "Maybe."

By then, the jitney driver and a burly man wearing a grubby apron were unloading the trunks and valises bound to the roof of the dented gray vehicle so that two other men could stow them away again in Mr. Middlebrook's spare wagon.

Mr. Middlebrook, for his part, had withdrawn a little way, and Lizbet, temporarily resigned, situated herself in the rear seat of the surrey, with Frankie on her left and Jubal on her right.

William, no longer playing the devoted stepfather, glared at her over one shoulder as he and Marietta and Mr. Middlebrook settled into the seat ahead of the one she and the children occupied.

Lizbet had never liked her stepfather; he'd drained away her mother's considerable inheritance for one thing, but the antipathy ran far deeper than that. William's greatest sin, in her view, which she knew was unfair, was not being Luke Fontaine. Her father had been a wonderful man, solid, good-natured and fair-minded.

A fine doctor, in fact, well loved by his patients, as well as his wife and daughter.

He'd died of a heart ailment when Lizbet, her parents' only child, was twelve years old, and the deep, echoing chasm his death had opened in the core of Lizbet's being had never closed.

Devastated, confused and blind with grief, her mother, Gwendolyn, had soon married William Keller, an acquaintance of Lizbet's father, and not long after that, Frankie came along, followed three years later by Jubal.

Gwendolyn Keller had loved her children, there was no question about that. But she'd never really recovered from losing Luke, the great love of her life.

Gone was the strong, spirited, incredibly intelligent woman Lizbet had known and dearly loved. It was as though marriage to William had drained her not only of her money, but of her identity.

Snapping herself back to the present moment, Lizbet glared back at William, half-sick with the remembrance of all he'd done to weaken her once-vibrant mother.

What was he up to now?

She was beginning to realize that she already knew the answer to that question, but she wasn't up to a confrontation.

Not yet.

Now she simply stared back at him, her mouth tight and her backbone stiff.

"Where are we going, Lizbet?" Jubal asked, scrambling onto his knees on the surrey seat, so he could whisper into her ear. "Who is that man?" He nodded in Henry Middlebrook's direction.

Frankie, blue eyes wide, face smudged, like Jubal's and her own, with the dust of the road, leaned forward and answered anxiously, "He's the devil, that's who!"

Fortunately, the noise of a team and surrey in motion, coupled with that of the wagon rolling along behind them, loaded down with their baggage, made the conversation inaudible to the trio in front of them.

"He's *not*," Jubal protested. "The devil has horns and hooves and a long red tail with a pointy end!"

"Hush," Lizbet said, in an earnest whisper.

"I don't like him," Frankie insisted, folding her arms stubbornly in front of her chest.

Lizbet left her agreement unspoken and said instead, "Everything will work out, you'll see. And no more talk about the devil, if you please."

Would everything work out?

Yes.

Lizbet Fontaine ached with purpose. She would keep these children—and herself—safe from the threat Henry Middlebrook represented.

So help her God.

TWO

When Gabe reached the turnoff onto his property, his dog, a yellow-and-brown mutt with one permanently bent ear, which lent the animal an air of perpetual curiosity, raced toward the loaded wagon, barking wildly and causing the horses to toss their heads and prance a little, though they were pretty used to Hector's tail-wagging, bright-eyed bombardments.

As was his way, Hector leaped through the air like a circus performer and landed on the seat of the buckboard, scrabbling for purchase.

Gabe steadied him with one arm, drew back on the reins with the other, as much to calm the horses as to let the dog settle alongside him.

With a rueful sigh and a fragment of a smile—the best he could manage, these days—he ruffled Hector's dusty head.

Then he brought down the reins again, and the wagon rolled forward along the rutted way home.

Cottonwoods lined the road on either side, their plentiful, pale leaves shimmering like silver coins in the midday sunshine.

How Bonnie and Abigail had loved to see the leaves dance like that. Abigail would laugh her little girl laugh and clap her tiny hands, bouncing with joy at the sight, while Bonnie beamed with delighted love.

At the reminder of his late wife and daughter, both lost to influenza on the same terrible day, a little over three years back, fresh grief speared through Gabe, cold and narrow and sharp as the blade of a rapier.

The past enfolded him like a shadow, the way it often did.

He'd been a soldier for just a few months, Gabe had; never even seen real action, let alone crossed the ocean to fight.

He'd joined up, though, knowing he'd be drafted soon, and left home in the fall of 1915.

As hard as it was to leave, he loved his country—what it stood for more than what it did—and personal duty required him to stand up for freedom, wherever it was under threat, though he was under no illusion that America didn't have problems of its own that needed solving.

So he went, even though it meant abandoning Bonnie and their unborn child.

He'd wound up near Seattle, in a U.S. Army training camp, and during a routine exercise, Gabe had been shot in his right leg when another soldier's rifle misfired, and he'd nearly lost the limb entirely, once the infection set in. After he'd gone through several surgeries, recuperated the best he could and managed to overcome the infection, he'd been sent back home to Silver Hills, Montana, with an honorable discharge and a marked limp.

For him, the return had been bittersweet, both a blessing—because of Bonnie and Abigail, the child she was carrying at the time—and a source of profound regret. He knew war was ugly, and that he'd been spared a heap of bad memories, or even a gruesome death, but it bothered him that he'd had to leave the battle for other men to fight—men who loved their wives and families as much as he did, yet had to leave them behind.

Gabe tried to shake off the thickening shadows rallying at the edges of his mind as he drove the wagon toward the barn, but they only crept closer. Even the glaring light of a late-summer afternoon couldn't dispel them.

The big stone farmhouse, empty these days and nights, except for him and Hector, stood at the end of the long access road, looking sturdy and lonesome. Sometimes, in the small hours before sunrise, Gabe would have sworn he felt the whole place heave a great sigh, as if it were a living thing, pining for those who'd once thrived there.

As always happened when he'd been away, whether in town fetching supplies or out in the fields, where he grew wheat, potatoes and corn, Gabe felt his grief deepen by fathoms.

He set the buckboard's brake lever with his good leg—the left one—and slid an arm around Hector, just for a moment or two, as though he could draw strength from his furry companion.

Hector seemed to have enough good cheer for the both

of them, but today, after encountering Elizabeth Fontaine in front of the general store, Gabe was inexplicably shaken and more than a little confused.

He'd felt something shift in a bleak corner of his heart, just looking at her. Just the faintest whisper of hope, soft as the touch of a butterfly's wing.

Hope?

Gabe made a scoffing sound in the depths of his throat. He'd *buried* hope, right along with his wife and daughter, and there was nothing to do but endure whatever time he had left on this cruel, beautiful Earth.

He'd never loved any woman but Bonnie, and he never would.

They'd been linked, the two of them, since they were little kids just starting out, attending the same one-room schoolhouse—closed now that there was a more modern building in town—a mile or so farther down the road.

Gabe had loved Bonnie as a boy, and he loved her as a man.

Their brief years together had been the happiest time Gabe had ever known, though things had been hard in the beginning, like they were for most young couples.

Early in their marriage, they'd lived with Martin and Annabelle, Gabe's parents. They had been honest folks, hardworking and still in the prime of their lives, and they'd welcomed Bonnie into the family wholeheartedly.

Gabe had worked the farm with his father and, when

they could collar him long enough, with Gabe's younger brother, Finn.

Gabe's thoughts soured a little, as they did whenever Finn came to mind.

He was the classic prodigal son, Finn was, except that he'd never come home to be welcomed and feted with a well-fed calf.

Not even when both Martin and Annabelle had drowned, crossing the Flathead River by a horse-drawn ferry. According to witnesses, Annabelle had fallen overboard, and Martin had jumped in after her.

The currents had been too strong for both of them, and attempts to rescue them failed as well.

Bonnie and her uncomplicated love had been Gabe's salvation in those days, and he'd gradually recovered from the loss of his mother and father.

Finn, perhaps driven by his own grief, had kept his distance, basically withdrawn from what remained of his family—his only brother, Bonnie and little Abigail.

As boys, they'd been close, the two brothers, fishing together, riding horseback all over the sprawling farm and the land beyond. And Gabe had sorely missed Finn's company—especially after the deaths of his wife and daughter.

Except for an occasional telegram or a brief letter, there had been no word from Finn, and certainly no visits.

In fact, after receiving the designated share of their parents' financial bequests, Finn had wanted to sign his half of the farm over to Gabe, free and clear, and that just about rubbed Gabe raw whenever he thought about it.

The farm was as much Finn's as his; it was good, fertile land, worth holding on to, through good times and bad. When Finn had sent the document for Gabe's signature, he'd torn it in two, then tossed it into the fire for good measure.

Given time, Gabe had thought then, Finn might still come to his senses.

He might still come home to stay.

And he might not.

After all, it *did* seem that Finn had been interested in his inheritance and nothing else.

Yes, he missed his brother. But he was furious with Finn for taking off, too.

Now Gabe shook his head, hoping, for the moment at least, to send all thoughts about his younger brother away with the slight wind that had risen to spin up little twisters in the dirt.

Stopping in front of the large, weathered barn, he leaped down from the wagon seat, followed by Hector, and winced at the jolt to his injured leg. He set his teeth and waited out the flash of pain.

With his throat dry and constricted, Gabe tended to his duties.

He released the team from their harnesses and turned

them out into the pasture to graze and drink from the little stream that flowed down from the hills.

With Hector getting under his feet at almost every turn, Gabe unloaded the feed he'd bought at the general store—winter was coming, and he was stockpiling rations for the livestock—but when he was finished, he couldn't bring himself to head for the house.

It was just too damned empty, that place.

Two stories of echoing rooms.

His best friend, John Avery, the town blacksmith and volunteer preacher, had been urging him to either sell up and move to town or pull his head out of his backside and marry up with some nice woman, but Gabe shook his head again, as though John had been there and spoken aloud.

So, with the evening chores still a few hours in the future, Hector frolicking at his side, Gabe slowly made his way around the back of the barn and onto the path that led up the side of the nearest hillock, where the family cemetery stood in full sun, surrounded by more cottonwoods and a scattering of pine and Douglas fir.

There were almost a dozen graves there by now, but Gabe went straight to the one with the headstone he'd chiseled himself.

Bonnie was buried in that spot, and so was little Abigail, who'd been laid to rest in her mother's arms.

Gabe planted his feet and stood strong, determined not to sink to his knees as he'd done so many times before.

Hector, quiet now, settled into the soft, fragment grass alongside the stones that encircled the grave. A soft breeze ruffled the dog's coat, and he rested his muzzle on his front paws, watching Gabe with gentle eyes.

Gabe felt another hitch in his throat.

He rolled his head around in a circle, trying to ease the tightness in his neck and shoulders.

What, exactly, had he come here to say?

Nothing he hadn't said already, dozens, if not hundreds of times.

When Gabe's knees slackened, he didn't try to stay on his feet.

He knelt within that oblong arrangement of field stones, closed his eyes and rested his forehead against the marker, felt the words he'd hammered in himself, the words that haunted him.

> BONNIE TYLER WHITFIELD
> AND ABIGAIL SUSAN WHITFIELD,
> BELOVED WIFE AND DAUGHTER,
> TAKEN TOO SOON AND FOREVER MISSED.
> AUGUST 12, 1918

Nearby, Hector gave a sympathetic whimper. He'd been a pup when the epidemic of influenza reached this pastoral part of Montana, full of that singular joy that comes so naturally to some dogs, making Bonnie laugh by jumping up to grab sheets or skirts or trouser legs as she hung laundry on the clothesline, keeping constant watch over Abigail as she toddled around at her mother's feet, delighted by her canine playmate.

Gabe straightened, traced the words and numbers on the gravestone with the tip of one calloused finger, his throat tighter than before and the backs of his eyes scalding.

One day, there had been laughter, sunshine, a puppy celebrating the wonders of mere existence. Then suddenly, the fever struck, first in town, then on outlying ranches and farms.

Gabe had tried to protect his wife and daughter, kept them closeted away on the farm, stayed close by himself. But quarantine hadn't saved them.

They'd taken sick on the same morning, first Abigail, then Bonnie.

Gabe had gone for the doctor, but that, too had been fruitless.

Doc Holbrook had fallen ill himself and couldn't leave his bed.

Feeling utterly hopeless, Gabe had sat with Bonnie, held a delirious Abigail in his arms and rocked her beside the marriage bed, praying to a God who appeared to be occupied elsewhere. He'd bathed their foreheads in cool water, trying to bring the fever down.

After four days, they'd died, within minutes of each other.

First Bonnie, then Abigail.

Gabe had never been able to understand why he'd been spared the disease that took so many lives, both locally and all around the world, and he hardly counted survival as a blessing.

Now, face wet, Gabe pushed back from the gravestone and rose awkwardly to his feet.

Hector was immediately up and ready for whatever might happen next.

And as Gabe left the small cemetery and started down the hill, he thought he heard Bonnie's voice, soft and almost inaudible, in the breeze ruffling the shining leaves of the cottonwoods.

You promised, Gabe. You promised to live.

THREE

Henry Middlebrook's house was a brick monstrosity, reminiscent of the town bank—*his* bank—which he'd taken care to point out as they'd passed it minutes before, in his surrey.

Lizbet stared at the imposing structure, noticing that, except for a servant woman, who came out onto the elaborate whitewashed veranda to greet them, circumspect and clad in a black bombazine dress, there wasn't another living soul in evidence—no wife, no grown sons or daughters, not even a gardener.

The handsome barn, set at some distance from the mansion, seemed strangely empty as well, giving off the kind of soundless echo one felt rather than heard.

Even more unsettled than before, Lizbet turned her attention back to the housekeeper. She was middle-aged, with dark hair, streaked at the temples with gray. Over that funereal dress, she wore an immaculate white cap with ruffles around the brim and a matching apron so crisp that it must have been starched.

When the woman executed a half curtsy for Mr. Middlebrook, Lizbet actually recoiled, outwardly as well as inwardly, because William drew close to her and growled her name in a tone of clear warning.

Deliberately, he proceeded to unpeel Frankie and Jubal from Lizbet's sides and dragged them toward the house.

Marietta, Lizbet noted, at the periphery of her vision, was gazing at the grand house with a kind of speculative wonder, perhaps regretting that she was legally bound to William and could not pursue Mr. Middlebrook instead. She was at least twenty years William's junior, and the age gap between her and the banker was even wider.

Such trifles meant little to Marietta.

When Middlebrook waited to walk behind Lizbet, she quickened her step and caught up with her stepfather and the children.

The housekeeper stood to one side, there on the wide brick steps, watching—*assessing*, it seemed to Lizbet—as the visitors passed into the entryway.

Her given name, Lizbet would soon learn, was Ruth, though she preferred to be addressed as Mrs. Harriman. She was a widow, thin-lipped and proper, and it was her job to oversee domestic activities in that vast, echoing house.

The place made Lizbet think of the whitewashed sepulcher mentioned in the Bible, full of dry bones. If one were able to pick that house up and shake it, she reflected fancifully, it would definitely rattle.

Despite William's promise of weeks' duration that they

would stay at the Statehood Hotel, it soon became apparent that that wasn't going to happen. At least, not that first night.

Mrs. Harriman was quick to announce that she had prepared rooms for everyone.

While Mr. Middlebrook and William retreated into what was probably the old man's study, the former closing the double doors behind them, the housekeeper led the others up an ornate, curving staircase.

On the landing, which was large enough to hold a grandfather clock, two chairs and a settee, Mrs. Harriman turned to Marietta and smiled obsequiously.

"The guest suite will be yours and your husband's, Mrs. Keller," she told Marietta, whose expression relayed quite clearly that she wouldn't have expected anything less.

With her nose in the air, Marietta sailed down the long corridor behind the housekeeper, reminding Lizbet of a figurehead on a ship.

Lizbet and the children waited outside in the hallway while Marietta was shown her quarters. The pleasure in Marietta's voice was indication enough that she was more than appreciative.

She remained in the suite to await delivery of her trunks and cases, and, of course, William.

"And now for the children's rooms," Mrs. Harriman said, her expression unreadable, her jawline strangely edged in white.

Seeing that there was, for the moment, no way out of this enforced hospitality, Lizbet straightened her shoulders, lifted her chin and said, "I would prefer to share my room with the children."

Mrs. Harriman narrowed her nearly black eyes and studied Lizbet as though she had just sprung from a nest of vermin and might deliver a stinging bite at any moment. "That won't be necessary—" she began, but fell silent when both Jubal and Frankie snapped to Lizbet's sides as though magnetized.

"I want to stay with Lizbet," Jubal insisted, stubbornness gathering in his little face like a summer storm.

"Me, too," Frankie said.

"Come now, children," Mrs. Harriman said, at last recovering, at least partially, from her bout of stunned disapproval. "You're not babies anymore. You can't expect to be with Miss Fontaine every moment!"

Lizbet made up her mind in that precise moment that if the housekeeper persisted in this vein, she would take her brother and sister and march straight to Mrs. Ornetta Parkin's boarding house, across the street from the general store.

The walk would be a long one, but that would not deter her, weary as she was.

She had money—not a lot—but enough, some in her valise, some carefully stitched into the hem of her velvet coat.

Retrieving the latter, of course, would require both privacy and access to her clothing trunk, neither of which were options just then.

But still.

She waited.

Mrs. Harriman waited.

Frankie and Jubal clung to Lizbet, like monkeys gripping the trunk of a banana tree.

Finally, the housekeeper flung out her work-reddened hands and huffed out a concession. "Very well," she nearly spat. "If you want to sleep crowded together like a pack of stray dogs, so be it!"

With that, the woman turned and walked down the hallway to fling open another door.

"Here," she said tersely. "Make yourselves at home!"

"This isn't our home," said Frankie. "We don't live here."

Mrs. Harriman rested her hands on her hips and glared down at the child.

Frankie was not intimidated.

"Just go," Mrs. Harriman ordered tersely, with another brisk gesture.

The *get-out-of-my-sight* part went without saying.

"Why are we here?" Frankie asked quietly, once the three of them had entered the room they were to share for that night, at least. "Father said we would be staying at the Statehood Hotel while we were here."

Lizbet shook her head, looking around. "I really don't know."

The room was—well, there was only one word for it: *prissy*.

Practically everything in it boasted at least one ruffle— the spread and pillow covers and the canopy on the four-poster bed, the lace curtains covering the windows, the scatter rugs, the lampshades.

There was an interior door, near the bed, and Lizbet, frowning, crossed to it, tried the knob.

It was locked, possibly from the other side, and she found that disquieting.

A second interior door, however, led to a full bathroom, with a real bathtub, a wooden commode with a pull chain for flushing and a pedestal sink with gleaming brass spigots.

Frankie, who had followed Lizbet into the room, flipped a switch on the wall next to the entrance.

Light spilled from a bulb dangling so high overhead that Lizbet hadn't noticed it.

"Electricity," Frankie marveled. "Just like we had in St. Louis."

William had filled both children's heads with wild stories about the Great American West during the long journey, and they'd probably been expecting to stay in log cabins or, if captured, native teepees.

Lizbet made no comment. She wasn't surprised, having

seen the lamps in the other room, so she merely nodded at Frankie, giving a silent order, as she often did with both children.

Frankie switched off the power.

It was late afternoon, but there was still plenty of light.

A workman brought up some of the baggage about half an hour after Mrs. Harriman had deposited Lizbet and the children in the frilly, fussy room.

Lizbet had nothing against feminine decor, but there was something almost obscene about this room. It was like a nest, carefully feathered.

Or a lethal trap, hidden from sight under billows of silk and ribbon and lace.

Her glance moved to the door next to the bed.

"Where does that lead?" she asked the young, muscular man who had just brought in their bags, indicating the locked door that made her so uneasy.

The man, whose name was Tom, ran a sweaty hand through his mouse-colored hair, which could have done with a washing. "Can't say as I know for sure, Miss," he ventured, after some thought, "but my guess would be, given where it is in relation to the rest of the house, I mean, that this room adjoins Mr. Middlebrook's. He's got the whole front of the place, according to Mrs. Harriman." Once again, Tom shoved his hand through his hair, then added, apropos of nothing, as far as Lizbet could determine, "Wants me and Joe to wash all six of the second-floor windows before we get any deeper into the fall. That on top of all we got to do looking after the horses and the yard."

A tremor of real alarm had raced along the tops of Lizbet's arms, raising the small hairs as it went, at the first mention of a door leading from Mr. Middlebrook's room to this one.

She felt like a sparrow perched on the nose of a jackal. A very hungry one.

Tom said his goodbyes and left.

Lizbet looked around the room, found a plain wooden chair almost hidden in one corner and half carried, half dragged the heavy thing over to the interior door, tilted it onto two legs and wedged the high back beneath the doorknob.

Frankie and Jubal watched with crumpled foreheads as she turned from the task and dusted her hands together. It was a figurative gesture, given that she hadn't dirtied them.

"No questions," she said, damming the stream she saw headed her way. "Who's taking the first bath?"

"I am," Frankie said.

"I don't want a bath," Jubal said.

"Jubal Keller," Lizbet replied, gently stern, "you will *have* a bath, and that puts paid to the matter."

Jubal seemed to sag a little, inside his dusty clothes. He sat down on one of the rugs, folded his arms and jutted out his lower lip, but he didn't argue.

He knew when he was beaten.

So, feeling a little less tense, now that the door to Mr. Middlebrook's room was blocked, and having realized that the door leading to the hallway had a key hanging from the lock on a loop of twine, Lizbet helped Frankie run a warm bath, then opened valises until she'd found a clean change of clothing for both children and laid the small, crumpled garments out on the bed.

"Father wants to leave us here," Jubal announced, still sitting cross-legged on the floor.

Lizbet froze for a few seconds, then turned to look at her little brother. He was only five, but he was clever for his age. "What makes you say that?" she asked, once she'd caught her breath.

"I heard him talking to Marietta this morning, at that hotel where we stayed last night, while we were having breakfast. He said Frankie and me were his trump cards—" Jubal paused, frowning, most likely trying to work out what it meant to be a trump card. "And Marietta said if he thought she was going to raise Gwendolyn's brats, he was dead wrong, because she'd leave him first. And *he* said, real quick, that we could stay with you, then."

None of what Jubal said really surprised Lizbet; she'd been suspicious of her stepfather's intentions all along, but she needed a moment to process the statement just the same.

"Are we brats?" Jubal asked. "Me and Frankie?"

"Frankie and I," Lizbet corrected automatically. She was, after all, a teacher. "But no, you are *not* brats. You are very good children, and it was wrong of Marietta to say such an unkind thing."

"She doesn't like us," Jubal said. He sounded matter-of-fact, sad. He sighed the sigh of a much older person then and almost broke Lizbet's heart in the doing of it. "I guess that's all right, though, 'cause I don't like her right back. Frankie don't, either."

This time, Lizbet didn't correct the child.

She sank into the chair in front of the vanity table and patted her lap. "Come here and sit with me for a while," she said gently.

Jubal rose from the floor, crossed the room, and scrambled onto her lap. "I miss Mother," he said, resting his small head against Lizbet's breast bone.

Tears smarted in Lizbet's eyes. "So do I," she said.

And then they just sat together, little brother and big sister, taking shelter in the love they felt for each other.

When Frankie had finished her bath, it was Jubal's turn.

He didn't resist. Once Lizbet had rinsed the huge bathtub with water from a large pitcher standing on a shelf above the commode and then filled the tub again, she left him to undress in privacy and bathe himself.

Like Frankie, he was independent—except when it came to being alone with their father and Marietta. And both children were naturally wary of strangers.

By the time Lizbet's turn to bathe came around, the children were lying on the bed in their clean underthings, having fallen deeply asleep. The hot water had been used up, for the most part; she would have the long soak she yearned for another time.

In another place.

In the meantime, a hasty but thorough scrubbing would serve.

Once she had finished her bath and dried herself off, Lizbet donned a clean, if somewhat rumpled dress, taken from a valise, and brushed her hair vigorously in an effort to remove the road dust. Then she wound it into a single plait.

Over an hour had passed when she was summoned to dinner by Mrs. Harriman, who led her and the children silently to the massive, echoing dining room.

William and Marietta were already there, seated side by side and talking in earnest undertones with Mr. Middlebrook.

Mr. Middlebrook was the first to notice Lizbet's arrival, and he frowned when he saw the children. They were not clinging to the skirt of her dress, as they had done earlier in the day, nor were they plastered to her sides, but their caution was evident, just the same.

The old man's sharp gaze drifted past Lizbet to Mrs. Harriman, who lingered in the wide, arched doorway.

"I believe I gave you instructions, Ruth," Middlebrook said, with an edge to his tone, "to give the children their supper in the kitchen."

"That would be fine," Lizbet said, before Mrs. Harriman could rally from the rebuke and answer her employer. "The children and I will be happy to eat there, together."

Middlebrook's bushy brows lowered, and he frowned and glanced at William, who immediately tried to ease the moment.

"Elizabeth," William said, "the table has been set for adults. Frankie and Jubal will be perfectly all right having their meal elsewhere, and Mrs. Harriman will surely look after them."

Lizbet planted her feet, figuratively and literally, and said nothing. She felt heat climb her neck and pulse under her cheekbones.

William sighed, looking exhausted and far older than his forty-seven years. Marietta slipped her arm through his in a rare show of support and glowered at Lizbet.

Lizbet glowered back.

Henry Middlebrook, seated at the head of the table, sighed heavily. "Very well," he said, with a touch of bitterness. "Ruth, please bring place settings for the children. Tonight, we'll all dine together."

Was there a slight emphasis on the word *tonight*? As

though there would be *other* nights, during which this exception would not be made?

Lizbet grew more uneasy. So uneasy, in fact, that hungry as she was, she doubted she could choke down servings of roast beef, carrots and potatoes, waiting to be eaten.

Middlebrook made a great show of rising, rounding the end of the table, and drawing back Lizbet's chair, once again the gentleman.

Was he a chameleon, or a cobra?

Both, most likely.

"I trust you find your accommodations comfortable," he almost purred, when they were all settled, napkins spread in their laps.

Lizbet was seated on his right, like a—wife?

Surely not?

She thought of the connecting door upstairs, and the chair she'd wedged beneath the knob and said nothing at all, because if she'd allowed herself to speak, she would have said things that should not be said in front of children.

William, seated directly across the huge table, elbow to elbow with Marietta, gave her a look of combined exasperation and pleading.

Marietta was sitting with her head tilted back, admiring the enormous crystal chandelier sparkling above them. She'd definitely dressed for dinner, wearing a bright blue silk dress, sheer stockings and a twinkling headband with a fabric rose pinned to one side.

Marietta fancied herself a flapper.

A soon-to-be film star.

She probably expected to eclipse Mary Pickford.

"Mr. Middlebrook is a widower of many years," William said, in a tone of false pleasantry, clearly trying to appease his host, though he was addressing Lizbet.

"It's a lonely life," added Middlebrook, with a forlorn-sounding sigh. "My Eudora died years ago, and we never had any children."

"Elizabeth is *already* an old maid," Marietta piped up. She was thirty, but safely wed and thus inclined to be smug. "It's time she found a husband, before her insides shrivel and she can't have babies."

Lizbet's suspicions were confirmed in that moment, and, though she'd managed to keep it at bay until then, outraged panic swelled up inside her like an invisible geyser. It was all she could do not to shove back her chair, leap to her feet and run for the front door.

She might have done just that, if it hadn't been for Frankie and Jubal. Of course she couldn't abandon them.

So, instead of bolting, and after a poisonous glance at Marietta, who had her share of nerve talking about anyone *else's* ability to bear children, she folded her hands in her lap, sat up very straight and said calmly, "When—and if—I marry, I will choose my own husband."

"I'm not hungry," Jubal said, in a small voice.

"Neither am I," Frankie added.

"Eat your dinner!" William blurted, red in the face, and both children flinched.

Jubal began to cry, and Frankie put a protective arm around her brother's shoulders.

In that instant, Lizbet felt she might burst with love for the two of them, her small brother and sister, and she wanted to weep, too, though she didn't dare, as the others—Marietta, William and Henry Middlebrook—would surely interpret her tears as weakness.

She couldn't afford to let them see her cry, lest they pounce.

No. She must be strong. No matter what.

She drew several deep breaths, steadying herself, and forced herself to eat. She was going to need her strength.

Tonight, she had decided, she would sit up while the children slept and keep watch. Even though the door connecting her room to Middlebrook's was blocked, there was still the one opening onto the hallway.

She could lock that from the inside, but there were probably duplicate keys.

So she would guard herself and her brother and sister.

Tomorrow, at the first opportunity, the three of them would leave this dreadful house and pay Ornetta Parkin a visit.

FOUR

Ornetta was sitting on her front porch on that faintly chilly September morning, wrapped in her shawl and watching the town come alive as the doors of the bank and the saloon and the general store were opened to the day's business.

In the distance, the school bell rang, a shrill sound.

Clang-clang-clang.

A horse whinnied farther on up the road, and two mules, tied to the hitching rail in front of the saloon, commenced to bickering, nipping at each other, braying and trying to kick.

Smoke rolled and billowed from the chimney in John Avery's blacksmith shop, which stood on the property behind her own, and Ornetta heard his hammer striking the anvil, a steady beat that reminded her of music.

Doc Gannon passed by in his buggy, off to make a call on some ailing soul, Ornetta supposed, since he was heading away from his office above the general store, not toward it.

Spotting Ornetta, he smiled and tipped his hat to her. He was a handsome Easterner with a preference for privacy and quiet ways.

Ornetta lifted one work-worn hand in greeting.

She'd woken up even earlier than she usually did that morning, feeling all jumpy and brimming with a sense of expectation and challenge. She was an old woman, yes indeed, and it had been a long time since she'd anticipated—and feared—anything the way she did now.

What was it, coming at her from who-knew-what direction?

She didn't know for sure, but she reckoned she'd find out soon enough.

Her boarders, six of them, had passed out of the house one or two at a time, nodding and offering a kind word as they went by.

Sam Ernshaw, the bank clerk, Mrs. Ellie Moore, the elderly librarian, Miss Helen Denny, the schoolmarm, Miss Nelly Carlyle, who was Miss Helen's niece and worked at the Statehood Hotel, John Avery, the blacksmith-preacher and, finally, shy Stella MacIntosh, who worked in the general store by day and played the organ at church every Sunday.

Ornetta had wanted to reach out and clasp Stella's hand that morning as she hurried by, hold it tight for a few moments, just to let that poor young woman know she was among friends.

But she'd hesitated in the end, as she always did, because Stella, reticent as she was, would have flinched at Ornetta's touch, and not because Ornetta was colored, either. No, sir. It was because Stella MacIntosh, no older than twenty or so, was scared to death of something or somebody.

The girl was painfully timid and clearly alone in the world, and knowing that bruised Ornetta's all-too-tender heart.

Thinking of Stella, Ornetta shook her head sadly.

She was about to rise from her rocking chair and head on inside the house to help her granddaughter, Pearl, clear away the breakfast dishes, pump and carry water for the two copper boilers, one upstairs and one down, dust and make beds and air out rooms, when the copper-haired young woman she'd seen stepping down from the jitney the day before appeared at Ornetta's front gate, flanked by two young children.

Ornetta marveled at the suddenness of it; one moment, the woman hadn't been there, the next, she was, as if she'd been conjured, looking flushed and earnest and just a little bit frightened.

"Mr. Whitfield said to come to you, if we needed to," she blurted, clasping a bulging valise in one hand and the boy's hand in the other. She swallowed, raised her chin a notch, and she sounded breathless. Ornetta hadn't noticed that before, but when she spoke again, the matter was clear. "I can pay, of course," she rushed on. "And we'll share a room, the three of us."

Ornetta didn't actually have room to spare—the place was full—but this woman was obviously in need of help and shelter, and so were those precious children.

If they cleared out Pearl's room, she speculated silently, and Pearl moved in with her, they could make space.

"Come on inside," Ornetta said. "I'm Mrs. Ornetta Parkin, but you can just call me Ornetta if you're respectful about it."

"My name is Lizbet Fontaine," the young woman replied, stepping back so the little girl could work the latch on the gate, "and these are my sister and brother, Frankie and Jubal Keller."

"Come in, come in," Ornetta urged, standing now, holding the screened door wide open. "You can have some refreshments in the kitchen while Pearl—that's my granddaughter—and I prepare a room for you."

Lizbet Fontaine was beautiful, that was for sure. Taller than most women, but not so tall that she'd loom over a man or anything like that, and slender, with a trim waist and a shapely bosom.

Her skin was clear, her eyes cornflower blue.

The children resembled her, and for a moment Ornetta wondered if she'd given birth to them, despite her claim that they were her siblings.

But, no, Ornetta decided as they passed her, entering the house one by one—the boy, then the girl, then Miss Fontaine herself—she was not the kind to lie.

Ornetta led them through the front parlor with its stone fireplace, clean but worn rugs, oil-burning lamps and sturdy, plain furniture, through the dining room, where Pearl was stacking dirty plates, and then, finally, into the kitchen, where there was another, less formal table.

Pearl carried in the pile of plates and silverware, her look curious as she took in the new arrivals. The crockery rattled as she set her burden down on the long counter next to the big sink, and her lips moved, though no sound came out.

Poor Pearl had the mind of a small, wary child, but Ornetta loved her more than life. Her granddaughter was all the kin she had left, and these days, it took the both of them just to keep going.

"Pearl," Ornetta said, after indicating that the copper-haired woman and her brother and sister ought to sit down at the table, "leave those dishes for me to wash. I want you to go upstairs and move your things from your room to mine, so these good folks will have a place to stay. I'll come up in a little while and help you change the sheets and tidy up a bit."

Pearl, who was slight, with lighter skin than Ornetta's, said nothing. She just nodded once, twisting the front of her apron in both hands and then left the room.

Her heavy shoes went *clomp-clomp-clomp* on the bare wooden treads of the rear stairway. Those shoes were ugly and cumbersome, but they kept her crooked feet pointed straight ahead.

Ornetta smiled fondly as she stood at the sink, pumping water into a teakettle. "I hope you'll be patient with Pearl," she said. "Her mind isn't quite right, but she's got a fine heart."

Miss Fontaine half rose from her chair. "Of course," she agreed, flushing again. "But please let me do up those dishes for you."

As she crossed the room to place the kettle on the surface of the big old black stove with its shiny chrome trim, Ornetta placed a gentle hand on Miss Fontaine's shoulder and pressed her back into her chair.

"We'll take care of that, Pearl and me. We don't ask our tenants to wash dishes or do any other household chores. They're paying to live here and we want them to be comfortable."

Miss Fontaine nodded, but she'd gone a little pale, Ornetta thought, and she clasped her hands together on the tabletop so firmly that her knuckles were white.

It was then that Ornetta realized the dear thing hadn't slept well last night, and quite possibly for a number of nights before that.

She wanted to send her off to bed for a good, long rest and tuck her in like a child. Maybe even kiss her forehead.

"You want to tell me what brings you here?" Ornetta asked, once the tea was brewed and the children were consuming tall glasses of milk and putting away oatmeal cookies like there was no tomorrow.

The young woman looked even more uncomfortable and indicated the children with a slight nod of her head. "I'd rather speak with you privately, if that's all right."

"Of course it is," Ornetta said, because it was.

Sometimes it near broke her, this strange, sweet tenderness that came over her now and again, usually when she met a person who might be in trouble, and almost sent her straight to her knees.

It was love, she knew that, and it came when it would, all but swamping her with its strength.

The children grew restless, once they'd finished their cookies and milk, fidgeting in their chairs.

"I wonder if you'd like to see my birdbath," Ornetta stated with buoyant kindness, smiling at the little ones. They weren't as nervous as their elder sister, but there was an undercurrent of anxiety beneath their politeness. "Folks say it's lucky. They like to toss in a pebble and make a wish."

The boy's eyes widened, as did those of his sister.

They both turned to Miss Fontaine.

"Can we go out and see the birdbath, Lizbet?" the little girl asked hopefully.

"May we," Lizbet corrected, without much conviction.

"I want to make a wish," the boy pronounced.

Ornetta was already holding open the back door, her gaze resting on Lizbet Fontaine now. "There's plenty of room to play out there," she assured her new boarder, "and there's an eight-foot brick wall to keep them safe, too."

Miss Fontaine swallowed visibly, then nodded.

Ornetta waited while the children scurried past her, onto the porch and then into the yard. When they were alone, she and Lizbet, she returned to the table and refilled the other woman's teacup.

"You're very kind," said Lizbet Fontaine.

"I try to be," Ornetta answered. Upstairs, she could hear Pearl thumping around in her weighted shoes, busy at her task, and she felt her weary old heart swell a little at the thought of her dear girl.

"Would you mind calling me Lizbet?" The question was cautious, softly presented. But whatever was disturbing this woman, Ornetta thought, it wasn't shyness.

Lizbet was uncommonly strong, for all her hesitancy.

"If you'll call me Ornetta," she answered, with a corresponding nod.

"Thank you, Ornetta." Lizbet let out a long breath, and her shoulders slumped a little. Then she reached into the pocket of her simple cotton dress and produced a thin fold of currency. "I'll pay in advance for a month's stay."

Ornetta nodded, named a modest figure.

Lizbet counted out the money, gave it to Ornetta and stuffed the little that remained back into her pocket. "I hope to find work right away," she said.

For some reason she couldn't have explained, Ornetta thought not of likely employers for her boarder but of Gabe

Whitfield and that big, lonely old house of his, where he rattled around all by himself, except for his dog.

He was a sad man, having lost his wife, whom he'd adored, and their little daughter, both on the same day, but he was young and strong and handsome, too. It was past time for him to put the losses behind him, terrible as they were, and get on with things.

Take himself a wife.

Like Lizbet Fontaine. She'd suit him fine, and he'd suit her, too, if he'd just let go of the past.

"Who are you running away from, Lizbet Fontaine?" Ornetta asked, putting aside thoughts of Gabe for the time being. She figured she knew the answer, having seen Lizbet and the others hauled off in Henry Middlebrook's fancy surrey the day before.

Lizbet told her about Henry's echoing mansion, the bedroom that connected with his, and how, as it turned out, her stepfather expected her to *marry* that lecherous old coot.

No great wonder that she'd run away.

And if Henry Middlebrook or anybody else came for this lovely young woman—a teacher, she said—they'd have Ornetta Parkin to deal with.

Ornetta Parkin and her rusty old shotgun.

FIVE

୬

The early chores were done—feeding the horses and the old cow, Lucy, who no longer gave milk—and turning them out to spend the day grazing in the pasture. Gabe had scattered chicken feed for the hens and made sure the water pans were full, and now he had time on his hands.

Gabe did not like having time on his hands.

It was too easy to start thinking. Remembering.

So he was chopping wood by midmorning, even though he had enough to keep the house warm for several winters, hard ones, too. Blizzards be damned.

He heard the rattle of an approaching rig from beneath the long canopy of cottonwood trees, and Hector dashed in that direction, barking, not because he was any kind of watchdog, but out of pure, simple joy.

That dog loved company, but he had his favorites and his *non*-favorites, too. The last time Henry Middlebrook had come by in yet another fruitless attempt to buy the farm, Hector had latched on to the old man's coattail and darn near knocked him over before Gabe called him off.

Now Gabe buried the ax deep into the chopping block and straightened his back, wiped his sweating forehead with a shirtsleeve and waited.

Doc Gannon appeared, driving his buggy, his spritely pinto gelding hitched up and prancing like a show pony.

Doc—Max Gannon, MD—was in his midthirties, a few years older than Gabe, leanly built but strong, too. He'd grown up and gotten his medical education back East, in Maine, and he still had the accent.

Gabe had wondered, more than once, why a man with so much to offer could have ended up in remote Silver Hills, Montana, but he'd never asked. If Doc Gannon wanted to keep his private business private, well, that was something Gabe understood.

Gannon lifted one hand in greeting and touched the brim of his hat.

Gabe didn't smile—he'd all but forgotten how, to tell the truth—but he wasn't unhappy to see the other man. Max Gannon looked after sick or injured folks who couldn't pay his fee, right alongside those who could, and Gabe had never once seen him use that buggy whip jutting up beside the seat to make his horse hurry.

"Morning," Doc said, pulling up near the towering woodpile. "You expecting another ice age or something?"

Gabe made a gruff sound—let it pass for a laugh. "I ran out of things to do," he confessed. "Decided to chop more wood and maybe deliver some to the schoolhouse and the church and maybe Mrs. Parkin's place. She's too old for a chore like that, and Pearl's no great hand at it, either."

He hadn't actually planned ahead that far, but as soon as

the idea to share all that split pine and kindling occurred to him, he saw that it made sense.

Doc gave an approving nod. "That's good," he said.

"What brings you by, Doc?" Gabe asked. "Not that you're not welcome, or anything like that."

Doc chuckled. He had very blue eyes, reddish-brown hair and, like Gabe, he was clean-shaven.

In the next moment, the doctor's face turned serious. "I was out yonder, looking after the Severn kids. They're little demons, the pack of them, but they've been having stomach trouble, according to their mother. Probably because they don't get enough to eat a lot of the time."

Of course Gabe knew the Severns; they were neighbors and had been for a long time. Danny Severn, the present head of household, had been a scoundrel and a close friend of Gabe's brother, Finn's. They'd stirred up seven kinds of devilment, the two of them, back in their schooldays.

Danny, unlike his salt-of-the-earth ancestors, was a confirmed drunkard, and he'd let a perfectly good farm go to hell.

Ironically, he'd married Sarah Holden, Henry Middlebrook's pretty, well-spoken great-niece, who'd come out to Montana as a young girl, since her folks had both passed and she'd had no one else to turn to, and once she met up with Danny Severn, it was all over but the shoutin'. They ran off and got married over in Painted Pony Creek, then came back because Danny's pa, Zeke, was too old and too stove-up to run the farm anymore.

They'd seemed happy in the beginning, the two of them, and they'd started having babies right and left.

Old Henry, one of the richest men in Montana, was sour on the topic of his favorite nephew's child, his only living blood relative, and rumor had it that he'd cut her off without a penny, soon as she threw in with Danny.

Life was hard for the Severns now; damned hard. But on the rare occasions when Gabe had encountered Sarah, she'd seemed happy enough, and she was quite generous, too, given how poor she was.

She'd brought baskets of bread and eggs and, once, a cake, after Bonnie and Abigail died. She'd never knocked on the door or left a note; she'd just left the food on the top step and slunk away, across the field toward home.

"I'll take some meat and spuds over, if the kids are doing without," Gabe said, with a nod in the direction of his smokehouse, which held too much food for one man and a dog, no question about it.

"I think they're all right for now," Doc said, with a sigh. "Sarah told me Ornetta sent out a whole slew of canned goods. Peas and beans and even blackberry jam. Old as she is, she and that granddaughter of hers raise a lot of grub in that patch of dirt back of the house."

Gabe almost smiled, the way he had almost smiled at

Lizbet Fontaine after she'd climbed down from the jitney, but before he'd spotted Henry Middlebrook, circling like a buzzard.

"You meet the new people?" he asked, realizing he hoped for news and wondering why he gave a damn. "Those folks who got off the jitney yesterday?"

"Heard about them." Doc paused, shook his head, readjusted his hat, which was sweat stained and dusty. "That's all. Word around town is, Henry's gone and made some kind of investment deal with a fellow from St. Louis. Has a fancy wife, this stranger, two young children and a pretty stepdaughter of twenty or thereabouts. Spunky, from what I'm told."

At the mention of Lizbet Fontaine, Gabe felt the bottom of his stomach give way like a trapdoor falling open, swinging on its hinges.

Henry Middlebrook wanted a wife—everybody in that part of the state knew that—but the decent women he'd courted wouldn't have him, once he'd shown his true colors, for all his money and his grand house.

The one woman who would have married him in a heartbeat—his housekeeper, Ruth Harriman—evidently didn't meet his lofty standards.

Too lowly and too old, that seemed to be his opinion of the widow Harriman. She was a servant and she was well into middle age, though still a lot younger than Middlebrook himself.

Gabe turned his head, spat.

"Trouble coming," the doctor said. "I can smell it."

Gabe agreed. He allowed himself to picture Lizbet Fontaine and wanted to saddle one of the horses, ride to town and rescue her from that greedy old son of a bitch before he could pull the wool over her eyes.

He shook his head, aware all of a sudden that she might not *need* rescuing, and rubbed the back of his neck with one hand. It felt gritty, as well as moist.

No, he'd leave Miss Fontaine be, unless she asked for his help. Brief as their encounter had been, Gabe had quickly realized she was capable of taking care of herself.

Up to a point, anyhow.

If the day warmed up a little, later on, he'd head for the creek, peel off his clothes, wade in and empty a bucket or two over his head.

Despite the fact that he was sweating, though, there was a sharp snap in the air, a sure sign that summer was gone and autumn was at the gate.

It was that chill, along with his dislike for idleness, that had inspired him to chop wood he didn't need.

Other folks did, though, and he'd hitch up the buckboard and take them some, once he'd cooled off and cleaned up. He'd have an excuse for returning to town when he'd just been there the day before and done what he'd needed to do.

He wanted to visit a few places, see and talk to a few

people. Get the feel of nothing in particular and everything in general. Though in a way he didn't need to do that, because deep down he knew Doc Gannon was right.

Trouble wasn't just on the way; it had already arrived.

"Guess I'd better get back to town," the doctor said. "Jemima Tokey is due to have her little one anytime now."

Gabe nodded, anxious, now that he'd made up his mind, to wash up a little, change his shirt, hitch up the buckboard and load it with wood.

He'd make his first delivery at Ornetta's place, even though she seemed to disapprove of him, albeit with a certain politeness. She stared at him in church most Sundays, probably because he sat on the last bench, his back to the wall beside the door, never bowing his head for prayer or singing along when the ancient organ huffed out hymns.

He couldn't bring himself to tell her, or his friend, the blacksmith and stand-in preacher, John Avery, that he wouldn't have shown up at all if he hadn't thought his being there might help Bonnie and Abigail somehow, make it easier for them to settle in up there in Heaven.

Or maybe it was for a more selfish reason. Maybe he really wanted to make sure he could join them, when his own time came, because he wanted to be wherever they were.

For the time being, showing up on a Sunday morning and tossing a quarter into the collection plate was the best he could do, and if God was as good as John said, well, He'd understand.

Now Gabe waved a farewell to Doc as he drove away.

By then, he'd decided he wouldn't go to the creek after all; suddenly, he was in too much of a hurry for that. Instead, he'd sponge himself off in the house, put on clean duds and get to loading wood.

Thus decided, he went inside, heated some water on the kitchen stove and poured it into a basin. He took off his dirty shirt, washed his upper body with soap strong enough to take the hide off a buffalo, dried himself off with a thin towel and fetched himself a clean shirt from upstairs.

It was wrinkled, that shirt, and stiff enough to stand up on its own, but it had been laundered and hung out to dry in the fresh air, and it smelled good.

He made sure of that.

Next, he rounded up the horses—they were enjoying their pasture time and didn't come when he whistled for them. At least not the first time.

Soon enough, though, the buckboard was creaking under a load of split firewood, dried and seasoned, and the horses were hitched up and straining at the rigging.

Gabe usually didn't take Hector to town with him, for many reasons, but that day, the dog looked so hopeful, Gabe just couldn't leave him behind.

"Come on," he said, making room on the wagon seat.

Delighted, Hector made one of his grand leaps, and Gabe caught him, held him steady until he was settled.

This dog.

Gabe's throat tightened a little, picturing the Hector of three years back. A puppy then, the dog had settled himself on Bonnie and Abigail's grave whenever Gabe visited. He'd made a sad, whimpering sound when Gabe wept and, at night, when he forced himself to lie down in the bed he'd shared with Bonnie, the dog had climbed up, settled himself as close to Gabe's back as he could get and stayed there until morning.

After swallowing hard, Gabe brought the reins down on the horses' backs with a light slap, just hard enough to get their attention, and headed back to town.

SIX

༄

Lizbet watched from behind a curtain in one of the windows in Ornetta's front room as the matched team of horses pulling Henry Middlebrook's surrey stomped and whinnied to a stop in front of the house. Behind them, as it had been the day before, was a simple wagon, piled high with valises and trunks.

Lizbet offered a silent prayer of thanks that Frankie and Jubal were out back, out of sight, playing in Ornetta's yard. Ornetta herself had walked across the street to the general store only minutes earlier to see if her order of embroidery floss had come in yet.

Off in the distance, the engine of the approaching jitney could be heard, popping loudly, as if it ran on firecrackers and gunpowder instead of gasoline and oil.

Only Pearl, busy dusting the piano with fidgety slaps of a cleaning rag, remained nearby, and her eyes were enormous in her thin little face.

"Who's out there?" she asked, sounding scared.

"Just some folks about to leave town on the jitney," Lizbet answered, hoping the tremor in her throat hadn't come out in her voice. "No need to worry, Pearl."

No need to worry.

Inside, Lizbet was shaking as she bravely opened Ornetta's front door and stepped out onto the shaded porch.

A light breeze set Ornetta's chair to rocking, and somehow, Lizbet found that reassuring.

The man driving the surrey set the brake, leaned back in his seat and tugged his hat down over his eyes, arms folded across his chest.

William jumped from the rig, leaving Marietta fanning herself and sneering.

He came as far as the front gate, William did, but he made no move to open it, which was a relief—sort of.

There was every possibility that he'd come to collect the children—they were his, after all—and Lizbet knew she couldn't stop him from taking them away.

The thought of losing Frankie and Jubal nearly dissolved her, right there on Ornetta Parkin's porch, but she managed to gather every last shred of composure she possessed and stood with her chin up and her backbone straight.

And she waited.

William's too-handsome face was pale with rage, and a vein pulsed in a thin purple line across his forehead. "You, Elizabeth, have disgraced us!" he accused, without preamble. "Marietta and I are *humiliated*."

A spark of disdain set Lizbet's cheeks ablaze. *William and Marietta Keller disgraced? Humiliated? Unthinkable.*

"I'm not chattel, William," Lizbet heard herself say, as the man at the reins of the loaded wagon climbed down from his high perch and went around to the back. "I'm not a commodity you can trade away for your own purposes."

William spat. Resettled his hat, which was already dusty, even though he'd probably given it a thorough brushing before leaving Henry Middlebrook's stately home. His suit looked gritty, even from a distance.

"You could have been a wealthy woman," William said, wagging a finger at Lizbet. "You could have had *everything* you could possibly want, if only you weren't so damnably *stubborn*."

Marietta, who had somehow managed to evade the ever-present dust of the road, sat pristine and calm in her smart green dress, silk stockings, veiled hat and high-heeled shoes.

"What I *want*, William, is for me to decide. No one else." She spoke quietly, but with consummate dignity, encouraged and strengthened by her own words. "Not you and certainly not Mr. Middlebrook."

Just saying that awful man's name made her feel hunted, like some poor creature of the woods, set upon by foxes or even wolves.

She gave an involuntary shudder, remembering that connecting door and the threat it represented.

At once determined and terrified, she recalled her and the children's hasty escape from the Middlebrook mansion just a few hours before.

She had allowed the children to sleep in, blind-tired

herself after keeping watch through the long hours of night, which had been silent except for the ponderous hourly chimes of the longcase clock on the landing, and finally urged them to dress quickly and to behave quietly.

While they complied, sleepily, Lizbet stood beside the window, gazing out over the lawn and side garden, hoping to see Tom, the stable worker she'd met the day before, when he'd delivered some of her baggage, along with small cases labeled with the children's names.

Once last night's interminable dinner had ended and the children were asleep, she'd crept down the rear stairway, crossed the blessedly empty kitchen, and slipped outside as soundlessly as if she'd had no more substance than a ghost.

After some searching, she'd found Tom near the barn, sitting atop a fence railing, smoking a nasty-smelling cigar.

Praying she hadn't misjudged him earlier in the day, when he'd come to the room she and the children were sharing, lugging in their baggage from where he'd previously piled it—noisily—in the hallway, she approached. He'd seemed friendly enough then; maybe he'd even disapproved of that dreadful door linking the room she was meant to sleep in to Mr. Middlebrook's private quarters.

After making casual conversation for a few minutes, she'd taken a chance and asked if he would help her get away. Take her and Frankie and Jubal to Mrs. Parkin's boarding house in the morning.

Then she'd waited with her heart in her throat, afraid the man would say he was loyal to his employer and could not deceive him.

Instead, he'd pondered the question for a while, still smoking, then jumped nimbly down from the fence rail, dusting the legs of his rough trousers with loud slaps of his hands as he walked toward her.

"Ten dollars," he'd said decisively. "I'll take you to town tomorrow morning, after the boss man has gone off to the bank. He'll be busy countin' his money then." A pause. "Fair enough?"

Ten dollars was a fortune, but she was desperate.

So Lizbet had nodded, thinking of the small mountain of bags standing in the center of the guest room she'd just left. She had no idea where the rest of her things might be.

"About our things—"

"You just pack up what you need to get by for now," he'd interrupted, not unkindly, "and I'll bring the rest of your things around later. Tellin' you now, though, Mr. Middlebrook ain't gonna be happy to find you gone."

"He has no say over what I do," Lizbet had pointed out stiffly. This was a fragile situation, she knew, but that didn't mean she had to cater to Henry Middlebrook's wishes. "Are you going to drive us to town or not?"

The man had shoved a hand through his hair, looked away, looked back at Lizbet. "I'll drive you to town," he affirmed, "but I can't promise the boss won't come after you straightaway. He's up to something, him and that stepfather of yours."

Lizbet let that last remark pass; she knew it was true.

"What time will you come for us?"

"Around ten o'clock," he'd replied. "I know that's practically the middle of the day, but that old man likes a leisurely breakfast. Reads the newspapers, too. A whole stack of them. So we've got to wait until he's inside the bank and busy counting gold doubloons."

The inference—that Mr. Middlebrook was a pirate—was not lost on Lizbet, and she'd nearly smiled, but her position was far too precarious for that.

At ten o'clock the next morning—with William and Marietta engaged in an argument in their room, Mr. Middlebrook gone to the bank and Mrs. Harriman occupied in some other part of that vast place, the wagon drew up, bold as you please, right in front of the house.

Lizbet and the children, waiting behind a huge rosebush nearby, had hurried to climb on board.

Delighted, Frankie and Jubal had scrambled into the back, giggling as though they were playing a game.

Lizbet, grim-faced and afraid, had settled herself beside the driver, clutching the handle of her heavy valise in both hands and whispered, "Quickly!"

After a bumpy ride, during which Lizbet kept looking back over one shoulder, afraid there would be someone in pursuit, they reached the town without incident. Though she noticed that the driver kept to alleys and back roads, and, after collecting his ten dollars—probably almost as much as he earned in a month—he'd deposited the three of them a block from Ornetta's place and vanished almost immediately, after pointing them in the right direction.

And now, much later in the day, here was William.

Here was Marietta.

Here was the moment upon which the fate of her sister and brother turned. Go with their shallow father and uncaring stepmother, or stay here, in Silver Hills with her.

Lizbet. A woman with no job, no real home, no plans whatsoever, except to love Frankie and Jubal with her whole heart and keep them safe and well.

Would she be able to do that? Would she be strong enough?

Silver Hills was a small town, which meant opportunities for gainful employment were surely limited. What if she couldn't find work?

For now, they had a room at the boarding house, but Ornetta, kind as she was, would not be able to keep them if Lizbet's money ran out. What then?

And, on top of all that, Henry Middlebrook would still be here in the town he practically owned, unless she missed her guess.

He represented a continuous threat.

Lizbet's heart rose to her throat and all but shut off her breathing. But still she waited, in silence.

Finally, William threw up his hands in angry defeat.

"Stay here, then," he almost shouted. "Maybe you'll come to your senses and get married."

She said nothing, because anything she *could* have said would have been incendiary.

William started back toward the surrey, climbed in beside Marietta and sat, staring straight ahead, looking as though he might literally explode at any moment.

The surrey, with its spectacular team of horses, turned in a wide loop, narrowly missing a wagon that had just appeared at the periphery of Lizbet's vision.

She didn't glance in that direction.

She didn't move, even though her trunks and the children's stood like a small mountain on the wooden sidewalk near the front gate, left there by the driver of the buckboard. He was on the other side of the road now, in front of the general store, helping another man load William and Marietta's belongings onto the roof of the jitney.

For one long minute—maybe two—Lizbet did not move or speak. She simply watched through flurries of sun-glazed dust as the couple prepared to leave Silver Hills.

She had not dared ask the question uppermost in her mind: *What about the children?* She had not wanted to remind William of his son and daughter, lest he insist that they join him and his viper of a wife on the next leg of their journey.

Had that happened, Lizbet would have had little recourse but to accept his decision—or to ask if she mightn't go along with them, to California.

That request, she strongly suspected, would have been flatly denied.

It was, of course, possible—even likely—that William hadn't forgotten Frankie and Jubal at all; he'd never been especially close to them, had always chafed under the responsibility, though he'd been adept at hiding the fact when dealing with his more respectable business associates. Quite possibly, he simply didn't want to be bothered with them anymore, especially with Marietta's constant harping about the inconvenience they caused.

How they were too expensive, how they were a constant reminder that William had loved another woman, how they made it so very *difficult* to travel, to shop, to dine in fine restaurants, to see friends, to continue in her quest to become famous. The list was endless.

And William hadn't even *asked* about Frankie and Jubal.

As she stood there, watching the jitney depart, impossibly loud, firing puffs of smoke from its exhaust pipe like bullets, a seemingly infinite sadness swamped Lizbet, threatening to drown her very soul.

What kind of man could turn his back on his own children?

A heartless and selfish one, of course.

Although she was glad William hadn't taken Frankie and Jubal with him when he left, she wasn't sure she could ever forgive him for it.

She had finally managed to get herself moving toward the front gate and the sidewalk beyond, when Ornetta appeared on the other side, as if out of nowhere.

The woman had clearly crossed the street from the general store, but in all the dust and distraction of William's and Marietta's departure, Lizbet had failed to notice.

She started, pressed one hand to the base of her throat.

For the briefest second, Lizbet felt light-headed and unsteady on her feet.

Ornetta paused at the gate, a small parcel and a number of letters in her hands, and eyed the pile of luggage on the sidewalk.

"So they've gone," she said. "Did your stepfather and his wife take the little ones with them, Lizbet? I was in the back of the store, where the sewing things are, when the jitney left, so I didn't see any of the passengers."

Lizbet swallowed, shook her head.

Her eyes widened as the wagon she'd seen minutes earlier drew to a halt in front of the boarding house.

The driver was Gabe Whitfield.

For some ridiculous and unknown reason, the moment she met his steady gaze, Lizbet's throat tickled, and a tear slipped down her cheek.

SEVEN

Hector, a dog who seldom met a stranger, leaped down from the wagon seat and rushed to Ornetta, who was standing outside her front gate, winding himself around her skirts like an oversize cat and making a whining sound Gabe recognized as pure jubilation.

Lizbet—*Miss Fontaine*, he corrected himself silently—stood opposite Ornetta, looking as though she'd just been sucker punched. And maybe, judging by her pallor and the slight wobble of her lower lip, she had been.

The sight stirred something fiercely protective in Gabe, something dark and cold and very primitive.

"There now," Ornetta said, patting Lizbet's stooped shoulder. "He and that *woman* are gone now. Everything is going to be all right. You and me, we'll see to that."

Lizbet sniffled once, drew back her shoulders and managed the faintest flicker of a smile, along with a brief nod.

He and that woman are gone now.

What did *that* mean?

Curious, but well aware that whatever was going on here was none of his darn business, Gabe set the brake on the wagon, secured the reins and muttered a few words meant to reassure the horses.

Before he could think of anything to say—the understanding passing silently between the two women now seemed intimate in a way that meant he'd best keep quiet until one of them acknowledged him—the two young children he'd seen the day before came out the front door of that house like broncs sprung from a rodeo chute, their blue eyes wide and their faces pale, like Lizbet's.

Gabe found himself wanting to scoop those kids up, one in each arm, and promise them everything would be all right.

"They're gone?" the little girl asked, staring at Lizbet. She was slightly older than the boy, and at least a head taller, but she still looked so small and fragile, standing there on Ornetta's front porch, that Gabe's heart pinched. "Father and Marietta are *gone*?"

It was then that Gabe realized the child might have been relieved by this news, rather than hurt.

"They're gone," Lizbet confirmed, so quietly that Gabe almost didn't hear her over Hector's happy yips and Ornetta's gentle remonstrations to be a good dog and quiet down a bit.

The boy, still in short pants, looked broken somehow. A tear zigged and zagged its way down his small, dirt-smudged cheek. "Father didn't even say goodbye," he said, and the pinch in Gabe's heart became a fissure, widening by the moment.

Lizbet didn't reply to her brother's statement.

She simply opened her arms, and both children came hurtling toward her, striking her like logs plummeting off the steep end of a flume.

Ornetta, who had just opened the front gate and passed through it, instinctively reached out to steady Lizbet, but the impact of two flying children nearly sent both women toppling to the ground.

Gabe remained on the sidewalk, not entirely certain what he ought to do, if anything at all. He'd come by to drop off a load of firewood as a kindness to Ornetta and her granddaughter, and he was unprepared for such a storm of emotion.

Hector, typically, suffered no reluctance to join in.

He was square in the middle of the huddle, trying to lick the little boy's face, then the sister's.

Suddenly, the boy gave a peal of laughter that nearly doubled Gabe over, right there on Main Street. It reminded him so much of Abigail's little girl glee when she and Hector used to play rambunctious games on the farm.

Gabe squeezed his eyes shut tight for a few moments, the only way he knew to regain his equilibrium when grief ambushed him, as it so often did.

When he opened them again, Ornetta was watching him, not with pity, bless her soul, but with a kind of quiet recognition, as though she knew what he was feeling and wanted him to know she understood.

That made his throat tighten as painfully as if it were being wrung out like a wet cloth.

"How much are you asking for all that good firewood?" Ornetta asked, still watching him.

Behind her, Lizbet and the children had definitely cheered up; they were laughing and playing with the dog, their earlier sorrows forgotten evidently, at least for a while.

"One of your cherry pies would be just about right," Gabe answered, and the feeling of dislocation, of standing a couple of inches behind his own feet, lingered.

Ornetta chuckled richly and waved a dismissive but friendly hand at him.

"That wood's worth a lot more than one of my pies," she said. "But I'd be a fool to turn down a deal like that, now, wouldn't I? So thank you very much, Gabe Whitfield. You can unload it around back if you will, then come on inside for coffee and cake. I don't happen to have a cherry pie on hand, but I'll bring one to church on Sunday if that suits you."

Gabe nodded, tried for a smile and, once again, fell short. "That sounds good. Make sure you hand that pie over before the service starts, though, because I don't plan to share it."

Ornetta laughed outright. "I'll see that you don't have to, then," she said.

Maybe she didn't disapprove of his not participating in

church services after all, the way he'd thought she did. Maybe she'd guessed, in her quiet wisdom, that just showing up on a Sunday morning, clean-shaven and clad in good clothes, was a major accomplishment for him.

Again, Gabe nodded, and before he turned to climb back up onto the wagon seat, his gaze strayed in Lizbet's direction and caught on hers.

Quiet now, and circumspect, she looked faintly puzzled, but otherwise affable, though she obviously wasn't going to recover from the children's upset as quickly as they had. They were still frolicking with Hector in the grass of Ornetta's front yard, the three of them caught up in the kind of celebratory brawl meant for kids and dogs and no one else.

When Lizbet looked away, Gabe felt heat rise to his jawline and turned back to the wagon.

He was surprised, therefore, to find Lizbet waiting at the back gate about two minutes later, when he pulled up alongside the high brick wall surrounding that part of Ornetta's modest property.

Lizbet had pushed the gate open and when Gabe had the wagon stopped and the brake set, she stepped forward.

"It's kind of you to bring Ornetta firewood," she said. "The supply is running low, as you can see." She gestured toward the dwindling woodpile near the back porch. "Thank you," she added.

"No trouble," Gabe muttered, ducking his head briefly, feeling shy in a way he'd never been before. "Ornetta's a good woman. She's helped a lot of folks in this town."

With that, he commenced to loading wood into his arms and carrying it toward the pile.

Instead of heading inside the house, as Gabe supposed most women would have done at that point, Lizbet filled her own arms with chunks of seasoned pine and followed.

"You don't need to do that," Gabe said, when he passed her on the way back to the wagon for more wood.

"I think I do," she said, with the slightest impertinent lift of her chin. "Today has been very emotional, as you've surely noticed. When things like this happen, I need to do something—well—physical." She paused there, between one step and the next, and actually blushed. "I meant—"

For the first time in a very long while, Gabe surprised himself by grinning. By wanting to laugh out loud, in fact, though he managed to restrain himself, because the last thing he would have chosen to do just then was to scare Miss Lizbet Fontaine away.

"I know what you meant," he said. "Don't worry about it."

If he'd been under oath, though, he'd have had to admit that the word *physical*, as it related to this quietly beautiful woman, revved him up inside.

The ensuing reminder that he was still a flesh and blood

man, and not a specter haunting a graveyard, made Gabe glad his back was to Lizbet by then.

After that, they didn't speak.

They just went back and forth, carrying wood until the pile was high again and the bed of the wagon was empty.

Gabe was sweating by then, covered in dust and smelling of pitch and thinking he'd better sit on the back step to drink the coffee Ornetta had offered earlier. But Ornetta was having none of it.

She wasn't going to serve a guest on the back step like he was a stranger and a hobo, she announced, instead of a friend and neighbor.

So he went inside, holding the door for Lizbet before entering, and washed his hands and face at the basin Ornetta had ready for him. Lizbet disappeared right away, and he was oddly let down by that, but she came back soon enough, having done ablutions of her own in some other part of the house.

She'd scrubbed her cheeks pink, and damp tendrils of her strawberry blonde hair curled around her face.

He stood until she and Ornetta were both seated at the table, then he sat down directly across from Lizbet. A steaming mug of coffee awaited him, alongside a plate with a big slice of pound cake on it.

The kids, meanwhile, had gone to the backyard; Gabe could hear them playing with Hector.

That dog, Gabe thought, was probably in hog heaven.

The realization saddened him a little; he hadn't been the only one to miss Bonnie and Abigail. Poor Hector must have wondered—if he *could* wonder—where they'd gone.

Like Gabe himself, Hector had surely been lonely.

Gabe took a steadying sip of his coffee and told himself to stop inventing canine melodrama.

Quietly, he enjoyed his cake and coffee and studied Lizbet out of one corner of his eye as she and Ornetta chatted quietly about building a fire on the hearth in the front parlor that evening, after supper.

He thought about what a comfort a nice wood fire could be, especially now that the nights were turning chilly, and made up his mind to have one himself. After he'd unhitched the horses and fed them, herded the chickens back into their coop so the coyotes wouldn't get them, carried in some kindling, washed up again and eaten something, he'd get a nice blaze crackling in the front room fireplace.

Maybe read awhile.

There was still an element of loneliness in the idea, but Hector would be there, curled up at his feet, loyal dog that he was, and there was some comfort in that.

Half an hour later, they were back home, he and Hector, taking care of the end-of-the-day chores.

Gabe couldn't stop thinking about Lizbet Fontaine and the children; they were so vulnerable, all three of them.

He wanted to step in, help out somehow, but he had no idea what to do.

He was feeding the horses and old Lucy, the milkless cow, when Hector let out a sharp bark and raced out of the barn.

It took Gabe a moment to register the chortling approach of a motorcar.

Since there was only one of those in or near the town of Silver Hills, he knew the call wasn't likely to be a friendly one, like Doc Gannon's visit earlier in the day.

Henry Middlebrook sat behind the wheel of his Model T, belly bulging at the buttons of his fine waistcoat, dusty goggles lending him the appearance of a strange undersea creature scanning for prey.

Gabe swallowed an unaccountable burst of laughter and approached the vehicle, stood a few feet from Henry's door, arms folded, and waited.

Huffily, Henry removed the goggles, revealing white circles of clean skin surrounding his eyes, while the rest of his face, whiskers included, was grimy. "You stopped by Ornetta Parkin's place today," the old man said, with an accusing note in his voice.

Gabe shrugged slightly. "So I did," he replied. "Do you have a problem with that, Henry?"

Henry's chest puffed out, and he looked so much like a blowfish that Gabe almost expected bubbles to pop out of his mouth and float toward the sky.

Again, laughter rose into the back of his throat, but he didn't let it out.

"You are to stay away from Lizbet Fontaine," said Henry.

"Why's that?" Gabe asked lightly. "You giving the orders now, Henry?"

"Because she is mine," Henry blustered. "I have an arrangement with her stepfather and it *will* be honored!"

Gabe nearly rolled his eyes. "This is the United States, Henry, not medieval England or ancient Rome. These days, if you want a woman, you have to come to an agreement with *her*, not her stepfather or anybody else."

"She doesn't know what's good for her!" blustered Henry. "I can offer her *everything*—money, a grand home, travel—" Here, he paused, lip curled, pointedly taking in the house, the barn, the other outbuildings. "Sooner or later, she'll realize that." A pause. "I'm telling you to leave her be or suffer the consequences."

Not for the first time, Gabe was glad that the farm wasn't encumbered by a mortgage, like many of its neighbors. If it had been, this devious old banker might have had something to hold over his head.

He'd seen the old tyrant, when affronted, call in loans out of sheer meanness, closing businesses, putting families off their farms and ranches or out of their modest house in town.

Gabe wondered how the man could sleep at night.

"Send that dog away," Henry barked, puffing up again,

before Gabe could reply to his warning. "If it comes after me, I'll shoot it."

"You don't want to shoot my dog, Henry," Gabe said, in a tone so reasonable that it probably chapped the old man's hide. "You *really* and truly *do not* want to make that mistake."

"Are you threatening me, Whitfield?"

"I'm not the one who mentioned shooting the dog," Gabe replied evenly, calmly.

Hector, the subject of recent conversation, sat at Gabe's side now, hackles raised, teeth bared. A low, ominous growl rumbled from his throat.

"You'll stay clear of Lizbet Fontaine?" Henry's manner was still obstinate, but he'd lost some of his bluster. He reminded Gabe of a hot air balloon with a slow leak.

"Because you ordered me to?" Gabe asked. "Absolutely not."

Henry inflated again in the space of a moment, turned so red behind his mask of dirt that Gabe almost expected his elegant big-city hat to rise three inches from his skull on a blast of steam, like in the funny papers. "I'll say it again," he managed, when he'd regained a modicum of control. "I plan to make Miss Fontaine my wife, so stay away from her. There are firm agreements in place. Have I made myself clear?"

"Only too clear," Gabe replied, feeling his own temper stir at long last. His fists were bunched, and the core of his body was clenched, braced for battle. "Lizbet doesn't *want* to marry you, Henry. *That's* what's clear, given that, according to Ornetta, she and the children came to the boarding house to *get away* from you."

"She'll see reason eventually," Henry said, though not with the same confidence he'd shown before. "It's only a matter of time."

"*You* are the one who needs to see reason," Gabe told him quietly. "You're old enough to be her grandfather, for one thing, and you're mean as a snake for another. Quit while you're ahead, Henry—stop going after young women and find one your own age." A pause. "If you *can*. I don't reckon any of them would want you, either."

Henry glowered. His goggles had been hanging around his neck; now he tugged them back over his eyes with a furious motion of one hand. Since he hadn't bothered to wipe them off first, they were still coated with grime. "I warned you," he said.

The Model T was still running, and that was too bad, because Gabe would have enjoyed watching Henry cranking the contraption in order to start the thing up.

With a grand flourish, Henry made a dramatic three-point turn and drove away.

Gabe, watching him go, let out a long sigh of resignation.

For the first time in more than three years, the woman who filled his thoughts in those moments wasn't Bonnie.

It was Lizbet.

The old coot's threats notwithstanding, Gabe wasn't afraid for himself. As far as he was concerned, the worst thing that could happen to him—the deaths of his wife and daughter—already had.

Lizbet, on the other hand, was in a unique kind of danger.

Henry Middlebrook wasn't a man who allowed himself to fail—when he did, he denied it—and he was obviously hell-bent on making Lizbet his wife.

God help her.

EIGHT

∽

The attic room was barely larger than a closet, with only one bed and one very small window overlooking the backyard and the street behind Ornetta's house, where John Avery's blacksmith shop and livery stable dominated the landscape.

Fortunately, Lizbet thought, with a sigh, there were trees, too, those wonderful silver-leaved cottonwoods that shifted and sparkled in the daylight. Even now, in the early evening, they shimmered, as though lit from within.

They were everywhere, those cottonwood trees, and even though there was an active silver mine nearby—this, too, Lizbet had learned from Ornetta—the town had taken its name, Silver Hills, from the trees. No one in the community had gotten rich from the mine, though a good many locals worked there; it was owned by a family called Bettencourt, over in Painted Pony Creek.

What she needed to do now, she decided, was to stop gazing at the scenery, go downstairs and see what she could do to get her life and the children's lives moving in the right direction.

Frankie and Jubal were squabbling about something, and Lizbet left them to it. They needed to learn to work out their differences, and that wouldn't happen if she constantly intervened.

She'd met the other boarders, including Mr. Avery, the blacksmith and, as it happened, he was in the kitchen, leaning against a counter and sipping from a mugful of steaming coffee when Lizbet arrived.

She took a moment to admire him; John was a quiet man, with strong shoulders and muscular forearms, and Lizbet might have found him quite appealing, even though he had just put in a day's work and hadn't had a chance to clean up. If she hadn't been so taken with Gabe Whitfield—not just his looks, but his generous spirit, that is.

"Good afternoon," she said, in a cheerful tone. "How was your day?"

"Fair enough," John answered good-naturedly. "How was yours?"

"I spent it planning—or *trying* to, at least."

John raised a curious eyebrow, but said nothing.

"I need to find work, Mr. Avery. Or is it *Reverend* Avery?"

He smiled. "I'm just a self-appointed country preacher. I didn't go to divinity school." He paused, looking both modest and, somehow, profoundly secure. "What sort of work are you looking for?"

"I'm a teacher by profession," Lizbet replied. "But it's been made clear to me that Silver Hills has one school and needs only one teacher. Which it already has."

John thought for a few moments, took a few more sips from his mug. "You're willing to do something else?"

"Anything that isn't immoral," Lizbet replied, thinking of the Hard Luck Saloon, where there was seemingly a never-ending demand for dance-hall girls. Although these women weren't necessarily prostitutes, they went about bare legged, except for fishnet stockings, according to one of the other female boarders, and their necklines plunged.

Lizbet was no prude, but she wanted no part of parading around a grubby saloon in a getup designed to arouse a roomful of drunkards.

John nodded in apparent agreement and smiled. Although he was legendary for giving thunderous sermons on occasion, he was gentle, too. "What do you have in mind?"

"I'd be happy to clean houses or launder clothing or clerk in a store," she said, but at the moment, her thoughts weren't really on landing a paying job.

Her thoughts had already turned to Gabe.

She hesitated, and it must have been clear to John that she wanted ask questions, because he prompted her with another nod and a raising of his eyebrows.

"You were around," she ventured somewhat tenuously, "when Mr. Whitfield lost his family?"

John's expression turned sober. "Yes," he said. "It was a hard time for him, as you can imagine."

She considered the terrible sorrow Gabe carried. She'd sensed it the day before, though she hadn't been able to define it, when they first met in front of the general store after she had disembarked from the jitney.

Now she felt a deep need to know more, even though Gabe's business was his own, and none of hers.

"He hasn't recovered," she said, almost muttering the words.

Ornetta had told Lizbet a couple of hours before, while they were washing the supper dishes, how his wife and daughter had perished during the Spanish Flu epidemic of 1918.

Lizbet, like almost everyone else, had lost friends and relatives and several students to that dreadful pestilence, and she knew how the grief gouged out space in a person's soul and put down roots there.

"I don't know if Gabe will ever get over losing Bonnie and that sweet baby girl of theirs," Ornetta had commented, while she and Lizbet were setting the kitchen to rights. "But he needs to accept that they're gone and move on with his life. He's a good man, decent and honest right down to the marrow of his bones, and bless his soul, he has no earthly idea how handsome he is." She'd paused a moment there, drying a just-washed skillet with a dish towel. "Practically every unmarried woman is this town is after him, but he's apt to back off whenever one of them gets too close."

Lizbet had taken all that in, but it was still something of a jumble in her brain—she'd have to sort through it later.

Ornetta had been right, saying Gabe was a good man, though. That much was plain.

"He's come quite a way, Gabe has," John said, after the silence between them had stretched to the point of awkwardness. "It hasn't been easy, of course. He takes a few steps forward, falls a few steps back and then tries again. Gabe loved Bonnie very deeply, and that little girl was precious to him, of course." The minister/blacksmith paused, shook his head sadly. "Letting go takes time. A lot of it, usually."

Lizbet's mind drifted back again.

Earlier, after unloading the firewood—she wondered now if Gabe might have taken her help as an attempt to woo him, like the other women he shied away from, and felt a pang of embarrassment—he'd brought her and the children's baggage up from the sidewalk and piled all of it at one end of the tiny room.

There was kindness in Gabe Whitfield, as well as sorrow.

"I'd better go and wash up," John said, interrupting her reflections, though just briefly.

When he left the room, via the back stairway, Lizbet resumed her pondering, though she did manage to send it in another direction.

With supper long over, the house was settling down for the night, just like the people inside it.

Lizbet continued to review the day, as was her tendency. She was a person who mentally weighed and measured her experiences, and the people she encountered along the way, hoping to learn more about herself and others.

She had liked shy Sam Ernshaw, a bank clerk and therefore an employee of Henry Middlebrook. Sam hadn't said much at supper, but he'd offered to clear the table after the meal—chicken and dumplings—was over, though Ornetta had chased him off, flapping her apron at him good-naturedly and saying she didn't need some gosh-darned *man* under her feet.

Miss Ellie Moore, who ran the town library, was a sweet woman who, by her own admission, would rather read a book than breathe. She shared a room with her niece, Nelly, who was twenty years old, somewhere between plain and pretty, with a lively personality. She earned her living waiting tables and cleaning rooms at the Statehood Hotel, and she wanted a husband. It was obvious from the first that she had her cap set for Sam, who dodged her politely and carefully avoided any conversation beyond, "please pass the butter" and blushed whenever she looked his way.

Which was often.

John Avery hadn't been back from work in time for supper, and Lizbet had learned little about him during their chat in the kitchen, except that he was a loyal friend to Gabe.

A nice-looking man with light brown hair and blue eyes, muscular shoulders and forearms, and small burn scars on both hands, he was bound to make a good husband to the woman he planned to marry.

Much to Nelly's consternation, Mr. Avery was engaged to his childhood sweetheart, Mabel Dunsworthy, who lived with her parents in Illinois. She was a seamstress and milliner of considerable skill—again, this information was dispensed by Ornetta, who seemed to know a great deal about everybody—and both she and John were saving practically every cent they earned so that Mabel could join him in Montana and they could get married.

Stella MacIntosh, another boarder, worked in the general store by day and played the organ at church every Sunday for the grand sum of one silver dollar.

She was young, maybe still in her teens, and she'd said little during supper, though after the meal, in the front parlor, she'd read a chapter of *Great Expectations* to Frankie and Jubal, much to their delight, and seemed to enjoy the exchange as much as they did.

Stella was quite pretty, but, unlike Nelly, she was no extravert.

Ornetta's conclusion—and Lizbet agreed—was that the girl was "scared half to death," hiding from someone or something. She'd shown up in Silver Hills about a year earlier, jittery as a cat in a room full of swinging pendulums, and as far as anybody knew, she never sent or received letters. Never placed a call on the only telephone in town—it was right there in the store, along with the switchboard—except for the private one in Henry Middlebrook's office at the bank, and nobody used that but him.

Stella was a mystery, as far as Ornetta was concerned, and she probably needed somebody's help, though it wasn't likely she'd ask for it, given the way she kept things to herself.

Mulling all this over, Lizbet returned to the attic room.

Frankie and Jubal were already asleep, their little bodies pushed close against the wall, to make room for their big sister.

After performing her nightly ablutions in the upstairs bathroom, she had donned her favorite blue flannel nightgown and smiling a little now, decided that Ornetta wasn't going to solve the puzzle of Stella MacIntosh anytime soon.

Lizbet made up her mind to befriend the other woman, though she mustn't be hasty about it. Stella was anxious, painfully so, and Lizbet didn't want to be pushy.

Behind her, in the bed, Jubal stirred, raised himself onto one elbow. "Why didn't Father say goodbye?" he asked, in a loud whisper.

Lizbet's heart cracked a little.

Frankie, was still asleep, exhausted from hours of playing in the fresh September air with her brother and, for a while, Hector the dog.

Lizbet came and sat on the edge of the bed. It would be a tight fit, with the three of them sleeping there, but she didn't care, and neither did her brother and sister.

They were *together* and, for now, that was all that mattered.

Plus, sometimes a place was good just because it *wasn't* somewhere else—like Mr. Henry Middlebrook's mansion.

Ornetta's house wasn't fancy, but it was welcoming and comfortable, and Lizbet felt safe there, as did Jubal and Frankie.

Taking Jubal's small hand in hers, she whispered, "I'm sure your father didn't mean to leave without speaking to you and Frankie first. He seemed pretty overwrought to me."

"What's 'overwrought'?" Jubal asked, crinkling his little nose.

"Upset. Distracted."

"He never thinks about anybody but Marietta," the boy said.

Sadly, that was true, but it wasn't an idea Lizbet wanted to encourage in the boy. "Most likely," she said very quietly, not wanting to disturb Frankie, "he'll come back to get you and your sister, or send for you."

Privately, of course, Lizbet hoped for no such thing. She only wanted to reassure a little boy who'd just been abandoned in a strange new place by his only living parent.

"I don't *want* Father to come back," Jubal said, with some spirit. "I just thought it was mean that he didn't say goodbye."

Briefly, Lizbet closed her eyes and offered a silent prayer that William would decide to leave the children permanently in her care, so he could concentrate on keeping his wife happy and making his risky business deals.

She knew, though, that the prayer probably wouldn't be answered, if only because both Frankie and Jubal had small trust funds. Since his deals never seemed to work out—what actual agreement had he made with that awful Mr. Middlebrook?—and funds from selling his first wife's properties, jewelry and valuable paintings would surely run out, sooner rather than later, he would be looking for ways to increase his bank balance.

And when the money ran out, so would Marietta.

Too bad William hadn't divorced Marietta and then married *her* off to his alleged friend, Henry. Lizbet had seen the woman taking in the mansion and all its glittering contents, and she was pretty sure Marietta would have agreed to the bargain without hesitation.

In the next moment, Lizbet realized she'd been letting her thoughts wander—again—and leaned down to kiss her little brother on the forehead.

"It *was* unkind to leave without saying goodbye," she said, knowing Jubal was still waiting for a reply. "Your father shouldn't have done that. The thing is, you need to forgive William, Jubal, not for him, but for yourself. When you carry anger around for too long, it can turn your whole life sour."

Jubal's indigo blue eyes widened. "Really? My *whole* life?"

"Maybe not your whole life," Lizbet conceded, inwardly kicking herself for the exaggeration, "but a lot of time when you could be happy instead."

"I was *real* happy today, when Mr. Whitfield and Hector were here," Jubal told her, making one of his quick conversational turns and thus catching her off guard. "When we get our own house, can we get a dog?"

"It might be a while before we can move from here," Lizbet said, wondering, not for the first time, how she would find work in a town as small as Silver Hills. Miss Helen Denny, the schoolmarm, the last of her fellow boarders except for the children, had been a dour sort, rather like Mrs. Harriman at the Middlebrook mansion. And, as she had told John, the woman had made it plain, upon learning of Lizbet's profession at the supper table, that *one* teacher was all the town's one-room school required, thank you very much.

Jubal was persistent. "But when we *do* move, can we have a dog?"

This was tricky ground. Like her brother and sister, Lizbet loved dogs, cats and horses, but this was a promise she couldn't make, not until their situation was more stable.

"No promises," Lizbet said, but with a smile. "Suppose

we can't get a dog, for some reason we haven't even thought of yet? You'd be disappointed and sad, and so would I."

"But someday?" Jubal pressed, with a sleepy smile and then a yawn.

"Someday," Lizbet finally agreed.

At that, Jubal closed his eyes, still smiling, and drifted off to sleep again.

Lizbet remained where she was, ready to stretch out and sleep herself, but stuck on the distinct possibility that William *would* return to claim Jubal and Frankie.

She feared, in the deepest, sorest part of her heart, where she kept sweet memories of her mother and father and others that she'd lost, that she might lose these children, too. Forever.

William could take them from her with a word; the law was on his side.

What were her options? She'd been over them many times, ever since Marietta had convinced William to abandon their lives in St. Louis and take her to Hollywood, so she could become a film star, and they hadn't changed.

She could flee, move somewhere where William couldn't find her and the little ones, but she knew that wouldn't work.

William wasn't a rich man, but he had means, and he would pay some detective agency to locate her. Then, when she was inevitably found, he would take Jubal and

Frankie—and eventually their trust funds—and probably have Lizbet arrested for kidnapping.

No point in running away; she'd be no good to her siblings or anyone else, shut away in some dreadful prison.

She shuddered at the thought, then squeezed into bed, practically balancing herself on the edge of the mattress.

There was one other option; she could marry Henry Middlebrook, even though the mere thought of him touching her made her physically ill. And he would almost certainly send Frankie and Jubal away to some distant boarding school, where they would be unutterably lonely and even mistreated.

That wouldn't do, either.

For the time being, it seemed, Lizbet was stuck between the proverbial rock and hard place.

She sighed and closed her eyes.

And when she opened them again, the night was fading into the pink and gold glow of dawn, and her spirits rose to meet the new day.

NINE

September passed, then October, and all that time, Lizbet teetered between panic and hope.

Every night she worried—perhaps a letter would arrive from William the very next day, demanding that Frankie and Jubal be brought or sent to him or, worse yet, that he might come back to Silver Hills to claim them in person.

Every morning, however much she might have wanted to hide under the covers, she rose with the sun, determined not to frighten the children by allowing her own fears to show. Since the three of them had settled in at Ornetta's place, Frankie and Jubal were far less anxious than before, and they didn't cling to Lizbet nearly so much, but she knew they fretted in silence, just the same. And Jubal had occasional nightmares.

Whenever the jitney rolled into town, usually in midafternoon when the school day was over, they hid behind Ornetta's front room curtains to see who would step down from the noisy vehicle.

On the few days when Lizbet hadn't been out, scouring and rescouring the town for work—all to no avail—she'd kept a close eye on her brother and sister when the jitney arrived, in order to gauge their reactions.

Each time, the tension in their small, straight shoulders was clearly visible, and both of them stood with their lower lips caught in their teeth. Often they held their breaths as well.

For all that, the children had come to love living in Silver Hills, however cramped the quarters in their attic room, and they liked school—Jubal had entered first grade, though he was a year too young, and so far, he'd been doing well.

Both of them had made friends, and whenever Gabe Whitfield came to town, always on some practical errand, they waited in the yard for the customary exuberant visit from Hector.

They endured John Avery's long but insightful sermons every Sunday morning in church, though Lizbet had caught them sneaking out more than once, no doubt hoping Gabe's dog would be waiting in the back of his buckboard so they could play with him until the service ended.

Usually, he was there, eager to play.

She tried not to think about Henry Middlebrook and managed to avoid him, most of the time, though he had a tendency turn up in unexpected places and to hover around her, particularly after church, when the congregation broke into small groups to chat.

Sometimes she felt a prickle along her spine and turned to see him leering at her in a way that made her shudder.

Once, he'd even tried to call on her, appearing at Ornetta's front door with a bright bouquet composed of the season's late roses, a cluster of fragrant red, yellow and white. He'd asked after Lizbet, who had seen him coming down Main Street in his chortling automobile and raced upstairs, praying he hadn't spotted her before she made her getaway.

Ornetta had answered the door herself, and she hadn't needed to be told that Lizbet wasn't receiving callers—not *that* one, anyway—and she'd politely but firmly turned him away. He'd been so furious that he'd hurled the roses at Ornetta's feet, turned and stormed off.

Since then, he'd kept his distance, though she knew he watched her when the opportunity presented itself.

Lizbet's first concern, however, was the children.

She was glad they were feeling at home in the community—overall, it was a friendly place—they had adapted quickly, and that made her nervous. If William took them back to live with him and Marietta in Hollywood, or placed them in some faraway boarding school, leaving would be that much more painful for them.

They'd suffered so much already, losing their mother, leaving St. Louis and all it represented to them.

She was thinking these thoughts on a cold morning in early November, when she left the upstairs bathroom, where she washed and dressed before any of the other boarders were up and about, and nearly collided with a beaming Jubal in the corridor.

He was clad in his long nightshirt, his feet bare, hopping from one to another, since the floor was frosty, despite the stove and fireplace downstairs.

"Lizbet!" he cried, in a breathless burst of pure joy. *"It's snowing!"*

Smiling, Lizbet shushed her little brother and steered him gently back toward the three steps leading to the door of their attic room. "Quiet," she commanded in a whisper. "People are still sleeping!"

"But it's *Saturday*!" Jubal practically crowed. "There's no school! Why would *anybody* want to *sleep*?"

"Jubal Keller, keep your voice down," Lizbet insisted, hiding a smile, as they entered their room.

Frankie, still in her nightgown, was out of bed and standing at the small window overlooking the blacksmith's shop, squat and stalwart within its softly glimmering copse of cottonwood trees. Like Jubal, she was thrilled by this change in the weather.

"Isn't it beautiful?" the child marveled, and, in that moment, Frankie looked so much like their late mother, Gwendolyn, who had loved snow, that Lizbet felt a bittersweet pang.

"It is," Lizbet confirmed quietly.

Her mind was easing its way toward more practical matters, such as finding work, as fruitless as the search had been, before her funds ran out. There was still a decent sum hidden away in the hem of her special velvet evening coat, but it wouldn't take long to run through that, with rent to pay, for though Ornetta's rates were very reasonable, Frankie and Jubal were both growing out of last year's winter clothes, shoes and boots.

Jubal tugged at the sleeve of Lizbet's practical gray woolen dress. The sleeves were long and the hem reached to the middle of her shins; the garment was warm and serviceable, though hopelessly out-of-date.

"Pearl has a sled—she told me so," Jubal put in, almost breathless with excitement. "And she said we could borrow it sometime!"

"All the other kids will be out sledding today," Frankie added persuasively, probably sensing her older sister's hesitation. "The hill in back of the schoolhouse is perfect for it, and *everybody* will be there."

"The snow may not even be deep enough," Lizbet said, heading for the window to make her own determination. Both as a child with her father, and as an adult with her students, she'd loved sledding, so she wasn't averse to the sport.

It would be easy for one or both of them to get hurt, though.

"It's been snowing all night," Jubal argued, and a stubborn note had crept into his usually cheerful voice. "It's *got* to be deep enough."

"We'll see," Lizbet said. "In the meantime, hurry and wash up, both of you, and don't forget to clean your teeth.

Then get dressed and come downstairs as soon as you can. The kitchen will be warm."

With that, she turned to the small wall mirror Pearl had left behind when she'd moved in with her grandmother to accommodate Lizbet and the children, and silently assessed herself.

She was presentable, she decided, maybe even pretty on a good day, but no great beauty.

Why was Henry Middlebrook so set on pursuing her?

No answer came, so she sighed and went on with her preparations for the day ahead.

After she'd used and put away the boar-bristle brush, Lizbet braided her red-blond hair into a single long plait, then wound it into a coronet at the nape of her neck and pinned it securely in place.

Like her dress, her hairstyle was out of fashion, but Lizbet couldn't imagine herself with a bob that barely covered her ears.

It was fine for other women, but Lizbet wasn't the showy sort, like Marietta and her theater friends. She was, at heart, a schoolteacher, and she preferred to look like one.

Not that she was likely to get a chance to head up a classroom again anytime soon; Helen Denny, the present schoolmarm and Lizbet's fellow boarder, had made it plain that she wasn't going anywhere.

The woman had to be nearing seventy, if she hadn't

already arrived there, and she was tiny, with parchment-pale skin, age spots and shaky hands, and she needed thick eyeglasses to read.

What mattered, though, was the fact that Miss Denny was a very good teacher; she walked Frankie and Jubal home from school every afternoon, and many evenings she gave them extra lessons—which, remarkably, they enjoyed.

Once Helen had realized that Lizbet had not come to Silver Hills to replace her, thus taking away her livelihood, she'd been friendlier.

Often, after the supper dishes were done, she sat with Lizbet and Ornetta and sometimes Miss Ellie, the librarian, who was well along in years, too, and they chatted about various goings-on around town.

Ornetta, though a decade older than the two ladies, was spry and mischievous and always busy.

On that snowy morning, when Lizbet entered the kitchen, Frankie and Jubal were already at the table, dutifully eating their oatmeal while Ornetta bustled about, getting breakfast together for everyone else.

She greeted Lizbet with a warm smile. "Hope you've got a good sturdy coat," she said. Her gaze slipped over the plain frock her boarder was wearing, past the wrinkly black stockings to her plain black lace-up shoes. "Boots, too."

Lizbet smiled. "I do," she replied. "We used to live in St. Louis, remember?"

Ornetta pointed to the table, an implicit order for Lizbet to sit down.

Lizbet obeyed, though she didn't like being waited on by an elderly woman, seemingly tireless though she was. Whenever she protested, though, Ornetta bristled like a hen with a flock of chicks tucked under her wings.

Ornetta brought Lizbet a cup of strong, steaming-hot coffee, before ladling thick mush into a bowl for her.

Lizbet thanked her, sipped her coffee with appreciation and lifted her eyes to the ceiling as she heard the others moving about, getting ready for their own days.

"Where's Pearl?" Lizbet asked presently, curious because Ornetta's granddaughter was usually up by this time, her chores well underway.

"She's feeling poorly this morning," Ornetta said, and for the first time, Lizbet saw a hint of worry in the older woman's face and manner. "I'll go across the road in a while and see if Doc Gannon can't stop by and have a look at her."

"You think it's something serious?" Lizbet asked, setting down her spoon.

Ornetta shook her head. "I'm not sure," she replied, "but my Pearl is a delicate thing, and weather like this can make her achy all over."

Pearl was not a child; she was a woman in her fifties, but she was bony and thin and usually shy.

It struck Lizbet how vulnerable Ornetta's granddaughter was, and she felt a stab of anxiety.

"I'll call on Doc Gannon as soon as his office is open," Lizbet said firmly. "There is no reason why you should have to wade through all this snow just to cross the street, Ornetta."

Lizbet half expected a refusal, her landlady was so proud and strong-minded, but instead, Ornetta smiled and said, "I would appreciate that favor. Thank you very much, Lizbet."

"Can I ask Pearl to lend us her sled?" Jubal asked, turning to Ornetta, who was just taking away his mostly empty bowl of cereal. Being a child, he wasn't aware that this wasn't an appropriate time to make such a request.

"'May I,'" Lizbet corrected him. "Not 'can I.'"

"No need to ask," Ornetta told him, ignoring Lizbet. "It's out back in the shed, leaning against the wall. You and your sister might want to clean it up a little—it's been there a long while now. Runners might be rusty."

Undaunted, Frankie and Jubal were on their feet in a moment, faces shining with anticipation.

Lizbet took true delight in seeing them so happy, there in that warm, welcoming kitchen, their stomachs full of good, nourishing food, their eyes gleaming like blue beacons on a quiet sea.

They scampered upstairs to put on coats, boots, hats and mittens, and Lizbet apologized for the clatter they made in the process.

Ornetta chuckled and waved her off. "It's nice, having young ones around. I enjoy it."

Lizbet finished her breakfast, carried her bowl and coffee cup to the big metal sink and began washing them.

"I'd be happy to help you around the house today," she ventured, feeling oddly shy, even though Ornetta Parkin was already one of the best friends she'd ever had.

Women her own age back in St. Louis, the ones she'd known in Normal School, were mostly married now and had been for some time. They'd begun having children right away and found themselves too busy to sustain much of a friendship.

It wasn't that they didn't care; they simply hadn't had the time to spare, and gradually, they'd stopped issuing invitations *and* accepting them.

Lizbet hadn't fully realized until that moment, in the steamy comfort of Ornetta's kitchen, how lonely she'd been for the companionship of other women.

The thought choked her up and made her voice catch when she spoke again, because Ornetta hadn't replied to her offer of help.

"Of course I don't expect anything in return," she said. "Truly, I don't."

When she turned to look at Ornetta, Lizbet saw the she was drying her eyes with a lace handkerchief, plucked from the pocket of her long, old-fashioned dress.

"You deserve better than you've gotten, Lizbet Fontaine," Ornetta said. Then she glanced at the wall clock above the icebox. "See that you dress up warm, now, before you go fetch Doc Gannon."

Lizbet crossed the room, put her arms around Ornetta and gave her a gentle hug.

"I'll be on my way in five minutes," she said, heading for the rear staircase.

She met Jubal and Frankie halfway up, and both of them were bundled into their warmest clothes.

"We're going out to build a snowman," Frankie told her. "Miss Denny says nobody will be sledding until after lunch. There'll be a bonfire and everything!"

"Teacher's coming with us," Jubal answered, looking pleased. "She says things might get out of hand if there isn't an adult around to keep an eye on all of us."

Lizbet, who knew there would be a lot to do around the house with Pearl laid up sick, was relieved that the schoolteacher would be joining the children for the sledding party.

Fifteen minutes later, Frankie and Jubal were in the backyard, knee-deep in snow, with the stuff still coming down in flakes the size of chicken feathers, and Lizbet had put on her winter coat and a pair of boots and set out for the general store.

Dr. Maxwell Gannon, she knew, kept his office upstairs.

Entering the store, head down in a fruitless effort to protect her face from the snow, she collided with Gabe Whitfield.

He hadn't been by the boarding house for a while, and he kept to himself before, during and after church every Sunday, so it was a surprise to find herself in such close proximity.

He caught hold of her shoulders and steadied her.

"You're in quite a hurry," he said, with an almost-smile.

"Pearl's sick," Lizbet explained. Plodding through the knee-deep snow on Main Street had left her short of breath. "I came to fetch Doc Gannon. Do you know if he's around?"

Gabe's gray gaze swept from her face to the boarding house and back again. "I met him on the road on my way to town," he replied, his expression serious now. "He was on his way to old Mrs. Jarvis's place. She's down with her rheumatism."

Lizbet felt a great upsweep of despair. "Oh," she said, utterly deflated.

Suddenly, to her vast embarrassment, she began to cry.

She'd thought she was in better control of her emotions, but between not finding a job, Henry's near-constant lurking, the threat of William taking the children away from her and now poor, sweet Pearl falling sick, it was all too much.

Gabe's strong hands tightened on her shoulders, though

his grasp was light, without pressure. "Hey," he said, gruffly sympathetic, easing her into the shelter of the store and out of the snowstorm, which was fast becoming a blizzard, "I'll catch up with him. Tell him he needs to come and see to Pearl as soon as he can. Will that help?"

There was something so tender in his deep, masculine voice.

Lizbet sniffled, dried her eyes with the backs of her gloved hands and, somehow, worked up a smile. Although the delay might be a long one, depending upon Mrs. Jarvis's condition, the doctor would know he was needed at Ornetta's house, too.

"Thank you," she said. She looked around then, as though expecting to see Hector somewhere among the dry goods on display at the front of the store. "You came to town without your dog?"

"Yes. I rode in on horseback—figured the wagon would get stuck for sure. Hector's at home, holding down the fort."

Lizbet nodded awkwardly. Strangely, she wanted to stay right where she was, face-to-face with Gabe Whitfield, but of course, that wasn't feasible.

She'd said goodbye and was turning to drag herself back through the ever-deepening snow, when Gabe startled her so much that she couldn't speak.

He swept her up in his arms and carried her right

across the street, his strides long and confident, despite his limp.

Something shifted in the very center of Lizbet's heart, and after a moment or so, she realized what had happened; she'd glimpsed a spark of hope behind all that weary sorrow in Gabe's gray eyes.

TEN

Why hadn't he kissed Lizbet when he had the chance, Gabe wondered, as he rode his bay gelding, Shadrach, through the stinging blast of snow practically blinding him and making him shiver, even in his heavy winter coat.

Shadrach was high-stepping, and the going was slow, and Gabe kept right on thinking of Lizbet, how sweet she'd looked, standing there in her bad-weather getup with tears magnifying her impossibly blue eyes.

Carrying her across the street from the general store to Ornetta Parkin's front gate had been an impulse, and it had stirred him up inside, set things to spinning and tilting every which way.

He'd been unable to catch his breath, at first, or even speak.

Given that he'd already made a damn fool of himself, he should have just gone for broke and kissed Lizbet Fontaine like he meant business. Which he had.

He'd wanted to take Lizbet Fontaine in his arms and kiss her until her toes curled inside those blocky schoolmarm shoes of hers.

The whole thing was intriguing.

Disturbing, too.

He didn't *do* things like that, sweeping a woman off her feet, carrying her through deepening snow and then wanting to *kiss* her.

Even so, he regretted that he'd missed the chance.

Instead of saying something sensible when he set her down, he'd touched her wind-chilled cheek with the back of his hand, inwardly wrestling with the sudden, startling desire he'd felt, and then he'd just turned around and walked away, without saying a word.

Nearing the Jarvis place, where poor Minnie was suffering from a bout of rheumatism, Gabe met the doctor.

Like Gabe, Max Gannon was on horseback. Most likely, his buggy wouldn't have made it out of Silver Hills, given how deep the snow was.

The men guided their horses in close and still had to shout to be heard over the howling wind.

Gabe yelled to Doc that Pearl was sick, and Doc yelled back that he'd stop at Ornetta's as soon as he got back to town.

With that, they parted ways, traveling in opposite directions.

It took the better part of an hour to cover the distance between town and home, including the brief chat with the doctor along the way, and Gabe figured he and Shadrach were both about frozen solid.

Gabe's feet felt numb in his boots.

He put the horse away in the stall next to its partner,

Abednego, checked their water and made sure they had plenty of feed. Shadrach got an extra scoop of grain for making the long slog in bad weather.

Gabe stopped to pat Lucy, the old cow who'd stopped giving milk six months before. She was useless, for all practical intents and purposes, but she was also a living creature who'd served his family well for years. He couldn't bring himself to put the animal down.

For the time being, he meant to go on buying butter and what little milk he used from a neighbor, Susan Henderson.

With his head down, Gabe fought his way from the barn to the house, wondering if he ought to string a rope between the two buildings, give himself something to hold on to as he went back and forth.

There was a blizzard brewing, and ranchers and farmers especially had been known to get lost in their own front yards, suffer frostbite or even freeze to death, depending how their luck ran.

When he let himself into the kitchen, though, Hector yipped and then leaped at Gabe as though he'd never expected to see him again.

Stiff with cold, Gabe took the time to greet the dog properly, then, after Hector had calmed down a little, he shook out his hat over the sink, peeled off his gloves and then his coat.

The fire in the cookstove had gone out, so he built

a new one, his motions slow and awkward as his fingers came back to life.

Once the fire was going strong, Gabe brewed some coffee, poured a mugful and sat down at the battered old table to wait out the thawing process.

He realized too late that his boots were caked in snow and muck from the barn, and he'd been messing up the kitchen floor just by sitting there.

His mother would have protested, and so would Bonnie.

Both of them had taken a lot of pride in keeping a clean and tidy house.

Bonnie.

For a long time, he'd been able to picture her bustling around that kitchen, preparing meals, clearing up afterward, all the time telling him about her day, but today her image didn't come as quickly and clearly as before.

Gabe closed his eyes and braced himself against a wave of guilt.

He'd picked up another woman, square in the middle of town, and carried her across the road. And he'd wanted to kiss her afterward.

Hector whined and rested his muzzle on Gabe's right thigh.

Gabe opened his eyes, patted the dog's head.

If it hadn't been so cold outside, he'd have gone up to visit the grave, told Bonnie he was sorry.

But *was* he sorry?

No, he was surprised to realize.

No, his only real regret was that he hadn't followed through and kissed Lizbet soundly, right there in front of God and everybody.

Frustrated with himself, Gabe shoved a hand through his wet hair and swore under his breath.

For a distraction, he stood up and walked over to the sink, kicked off his boots and foot-shoved them beside the back door, where they belonged.

Then he turned his attention to the window above the sink, coffee mug still in his left hand, and watched the snow. It had slackened off a little, though long experience told him that was temporary, and if he wanted to run a line between the house and the barn, he'd better do it right away.

Having made that decision, Gabe put his coat and boots back on, leaving his gloves to dry near the stove, and set out for the barn.

This time, Hector came with him.

While he was searching for the long rope he kept for just this purpose, as had his father and grandfather before him, he came across a forgotten project, one he hadn't been able to bear looking at after Bonnie and Abigail died.

He could make out the shape under the dusty old tarp covering it, and his throat instantly tightened.

With a trembling hand, Gabe reached out and uncovered the sizable dollhouse he'd been building for Abigail, back when she was still alive and healthy. He'd planned to finish the miniature structure and put it under the tree on Christmas Eve for his little girl to find the next morning.

He swallowed hard, and Hector whimpered again, sensing his sorrow.

And there *was* still sorrow, you bet there was, but there was something else, too. A certain quiet, slowly expanding joy.

He thought of Frankie, Lizbet's kid sister, and her small brother.

He'd seen them a few days before, standing in front of the general store, gazing through the frosted window at a display of toys—dolls, wagons, sleds, building blocks—all the enticements of childhood Christmases.

They'd seemed so wistful, the pair of them, that Gabe, in town to fetch his mail, had felt a pang in the area of his heart.

Now, there in his kitchen, Gabe pictured Frankie playing with the elaborate dollhouse he'd built, moving the small pieces of furniture he'd carved, the rugs and curtains Bonnie had stitched together.

Gabe knew Lizbet was low on money, if she had any at all—it hadn't been a stretch to figure that out. Practically everybody in town knew she'd been looking for work for weeks, visiting the same places over and over again and being turned away each time.

A muscle tightened in Gabe's jaw as he thought of her stepfather, and how he'd abandoned her and the little ones in an unfamiliar town, probably with little or no money; Ornetta had told him a thing or two about William Keller, and he hadn't liked what he'd heard.

No doubt Keller had wanted to punish her for refusing to marry old man Middlebrook. Something about a deal going sour, Ornetta said, and though that was just a rumor, Sam Ernshaw, one of Ornetta's boarders, had mentioned a financial fiasco in passing, and he might have been in a position to know. After all, the man worked for Middlebrook, right there in the bank.

It was the town's *only* bank, in fact, which was why Gabe and several other people, including his best friend, John Avery, rode over to Painted Pony Creek to make their deposits and withdrawals in another establishment.

John earned next to nothing preaching, but he was the only blacksmith for miles around, which meant he did a lot of business.

Buoyed by the thought of making a child happy, Gabe sighed covered the dollhouse up again.

It was a while 'til Christmas; maybe he'd finish it—wash it down, give it a coat of paint, maybe block off a few more tiny rooms and carve more furniture.

A thing like that ought to be giving someone joy, not wasting away in a barn, and Gabe had worked hard on it.

He'd make sure there was something for the boy, too. A wagon, maybe. Or a sled.

The decision made, Gabe gathered the rope from its

hook on the wall, looped it around one bare hand and told Hector, "Let's get this done before it gets dark."

The job was an awkward one—the chill in his hands made him fumble quite a bit—but after roughly half an hour, during which the storm was rapidly gathering momentum, it was done. The rope stretched taut, waist-high, from the barn to the house, securely tied at both ends.

Gabe looked in on the chickens—they were huddled together in their sturdy coop and clucking a lot after they spotted Hector in the doorway, but otherwise they were doing fine, like the horses and the cow.

Back in the house, Gabe built the fire up again, wrangled some pots and pans from the cupboards next to the sink and fried up a hefty meal of ham and eggs. Like always, he shared the bounty with Hector, who clearly appreciated the gesture.

After he'd eaten and put the kitchen to rights again, Gabe lit an oil lamp—it was still fairly early, but the storm was swallowing up whatever light there was—and sat back down at the table to read the mail he'd ridden into town to fetch.

Of all things, there was a letter from Henry Middlebrook, which surprised him. Nobody reading it would have suspected that the greedy old codger had ever butted heads with Gabe.

It was friendly, that letter, to the point of being smarmy. Henry wanted to buy the mineral rights to the Whitfield farm—old news—and commence mining for silver. He offered to compensate Gabe handsomely, in addition to the purchase, should his crews strike paydirt.

Gabe sighed and set the letter aside.

He didn't want his land stripped and gouged and gutted, and although he wasn't a rich man by any means, Gabe had no real interest in building wealth. Furthermore, even if he *had* been willing to make such an agreement, he wouldn't have chosen Middlebrook to be on the receiving end.

He had all the money he needed, and some put away against hard times.

The house was livable—he'd put on a new roof over the summer—and the barn was as solid as old Noah's ark, and he had no call, or desire, to wear fancy clothes like old Henry.

Nor did he want an automobile, unlike practically everybody else he knew. They were loud, and too much trouble in the bargain, always breaking down alongside the road or flinging up dirt and mud from all four wheels.

Feeling particularly lonely, now that the chores were done and the dishes had been washed and put back in their places and he had nothing much to keep himself occupied, he turned his attention back to the mail again.

He found several advertisements for farming equipment and the like, none of which interested him, a statement from his bank—and a letter from his younger brother, Finn.

There was no return address, but the envelope was postmarked Seattle and dated nearly two weeks back.

Gabe was at once pleased and wary.

He and Finn weren't exactly estranged, but they weren't close like a lot of other brothers, either. Not anymore.

Though good-natured, Finn had been three kinds of a hell-raiser growing up, and he'd caused their parents—and Gabe himself—plenty of trouble.

When their parents died, Finn hadn't come home. He'd collected his share of the inheritance, by mail, and all but thrown away his share of the farm.

If Finn had grieved over losing their mother and father, he'd never given any indication of it. And worse, as far as Gabe was concerned, he hadn't even responded when Gabe wrote to tell him that Bonnie and Abigail were gone.

With all that in mind, Gabe took his time opening the letter—it was one page, written in Finn's familiar cramped hand, slanting to the left—and the brief message made Gabe want to crumple the thing and toss it into the fire.

I'm coming home, Finn had scrawled. *We have a lot of things to iron out, you and me.*

Well, Gabe thought, with a mixture of hope and irritation, you're right about that much anyway.

ELEVEN

༄

When Dr. Maxwell Gannon knocked on Ornetta's door that wickedly cold and impossibly snowy afternoon, Lizbet let him in.

Ornetta was upstairs with Pearl, bathing the younger woman's forehead in an attempt to bring down her rising fever and praying aloud for God's intervention.

Lizbet had been praying, too, although silently.

Frankie and Jubal, disappointed that the weather was too bad even for sledding, sat across from each other on the floor in front of the crackling fireplace, solemnly engaged in a game of jacks.

Like everyone else in the house, they were worried about Pearl.

Ornetta had strictly forbidden all the boarders, Lizbet included, to go near her granddaughter, in case of contagion, so she led the doctor onto the second-floor landing and pointed out Ornetta's room.

Grimly concerned, the doctor nodded, started in that direction, then stopped and turned back to Lizbet. His coat and hat were laden with snow, and his handsome face was red with cold.

Wordlessly, Lizbet reached out, and he handed over the

hat and coat, shuffling his battered medical bag from one hand to the other in the process.

"Is anyone else in the house ailing?" he asked, his voice low. Although she'd seen Doc Gannon from a distance, this was the first time she'd been close enough for a conversation.

With a flush warming her cheeks, she wondered if he'd heard about her making a public spectacle of herself earlier, letting Gabe Whitfield carry her across Main Street in the broad light of day.

Lizbet returned her attention to where it belonged. "No one has said they felt sick," she replied, musing. Most of the boarders were at home because of the storm, keeping to their rooms.

Shy Stella MacIntosh had come downstairs a few hours before, when Lizbet rang the lunch bell to invite the others to the dining room, quietly thanked Lizbet for preparing the meal—a simple one of egg salad sandwiches and canned peaches from Ornetta's store of jars in the pantry—and sat down to eat in silence.

Miss Helen and Miss Ellie had soon appeared, as well; they'd been sitting together in Miss Ellie's room, embroidering samplers they planned to give as Christmas gifts.

Christmas. Lizbet hadn't wanted to *think* about the rapidly approaching holiday. Frankie was old enough to understand that there might be few if any presents that year, but Jubal, at five, still believed in St. Nicholas.

Sam had gone to the bank at midmorning, even though

it was the weekend, but he'd returned soon afterward, explaining that Mr. Middlebrook had decided not to open for the usual Saturday half day, due, of course, to the weather.

Nelly, too, had been sent home, since the Statehood Hotel was empty of guests, so there were no rooms to clean or meals to serve.

She'd brought a magazine back with her, purchased at the general store—one with a sketch of a saucy flapper on the cover, posing in a skimpy dress and holding an impossibly long cigarette holder in one hand.

Miss Helen, Nelly's aunt, with whom she shared a room, was offended by the publication. A peaceful accord had yet to be reached.

That left John Avery, the one boarder who wasn't present; as usual, he was in his blacksmith shop, hard at work.

Suddenly, Lizbet realized she'd gotten so caught up in reviewing who was in the house and who wasn't that she'd been standing there, she now realized, staring at the doctor for a full minute without saying anything.

He didn't seem troubled by that, however; he shifted his battered leather medical bag from one hand to the other, glanced back over his shoulder toward Ornetta's room, then met Lizbet's gaze and asked, "Was there something else, Miss—er—?"

"Lizbet," she replied. Then, deciding she'd sounded forward, she clarified, "Lizbet Fontaine. I'm new to Silver Hills."

The doctor was young, somewhere in his midthirties probably, but he looked much older as he shoved a hand through his dampened, sandy-colored hair.

Lizbet was struck by the thought that he was not only cold, but exhausted to the very marrow of his bones. After all, he was the only qualified physician for miles around.

"I'm Doc Gannon," he said, unnecessarily.

Lizbet merely nodded. "If you don't mind, I'll just wait here for a few moments, in case Ornetta needs something brought upstairs. I'm sure she would enjoy a cup of tea or coffee, and I don't believe she's eaten since breakfast."

Doc Gannon nodded back, and the merest hint of a smile lit his kind eyes. "That's very thoughtful. I'll let you know, one way or the other."

With that, he disappeared into Ornetta's room.

Lizbet heard the low mutter of voices, then, just as she was finally turning to go downstairs again, the door opened once more and Doc Gannon stuck his head out.

"Mrs. Parkin says coffee sounds good, and make it strong, please. She could eat a bowl of peaches or apricots, but that's all she wants for now." Inside the room, Ornetta said something Lizbet couldn't hear, and the doctor turned to listen, then turned back. "She says to get one of the men to haul up a couple of buckets of cold water. Colder the better."

"All right," Lizbet confirmed, ready to help in any way she could.

Downstairs, in the kitchen, she brewed a fresh pot of coffee, strong the way Ornetta liked it, laid a tray with two cups and saucers, spoons, a sturdy oversize teapot, a bowl of sugar cubes and a small pitcher of cream. Then she went into the pantry and brought out a jar of peach preserves, picked, pitted, washed and put up by Ornetta and Pearl, along with pears, apple slices, carrots, green beans, sliced beets and potatoes, all from their own backyard.

Lizbet put a serving of peaches into the prettiest bowl she could find and placed them on the tray.

When the coffee was ready, she filled the teapot with steaming hot brew and made her way carefully out of the kitchen and up the back stairs.

Reaching Ornetta's door and not wanting to set the heavy tray down to knock, she called out quietly, "Ornetta? It's me, Lizbet. I've brought your coffee and some peaches."

Doc Gannon answered, instead of Ornetta, stepping into the corridor and looking even more exhausted than before. He took the tray from Lizbet's hands and made an admirable attempt at a smile. "Thank you," he said.

Lizbet was at the kitchen sink, pumping icy cold water into the second of two buckets about fifteen minutes later—she'd paused to look through the pantry again, with an eye to making supper for the household—when the doctor descended the back stairway and entered the kitchen, carrying one coffee cup, now empty.

He smiled when he saw his coat draped over the back

of a chair pulled close to the cookstove to dry out, and his hat resting on a counter nearby.

"That was kind of you," he said. "I wasn't looking forward to putting that sopping wet coat back on, just to cross the street to my office."

"If you aren't in a hurry, sit down," Lizbet said quietly. "I'll pour you another cup of coffee and you can rest for a few minutes."

Instead of resting, Doc Gannon crossed to the sink, took up the two buckets, now brimming with cold water, one in each hand.

"I think it might be more suitable for *you* to sit down for a few minutes, Miss Fontaine, and rest while I take these buckets upstairs to Mrs. Parkin."

Lizbet didn't reply; she could see that Doc Gannon had a firm grip on the handles of both the water buckets and he wasn't going to allow her to carry them up to Ornetta, who would continue her attempts to bring Pearl's fever down.

When the doctor returned, she had already poured him a second cup of coffee and set it on the table, along with a slice of Ornetta's incomparable apple cake.

"How is Pearl?" she asked softly.

Doc Gannon sighed. Shook his head. "She's come down with pneumonia, I'm afraid. There's not much I can do, actually, except dose her with quinine, and I'm reluctant to do that."

"Sit down," Lizbet said.

He fell into a chair, reached for the coffee mug. Stopped and looked up at her. "Mine?" he asked, with a twinkle of weary mischief in his eyes.

"The cake, too," Lizbet replied, with a rather formal nod.

"Please take a chair, Miss Fontaine. I don't want to have to stand up again to drink this coffee, much as I need it, but I will if necessary."

Lizbet smiled cautiously, sat down across the table from him, with a cup of coffee for herself.

"Thank you," the doctor said, with relieved amusement.

"You're welcome," Lizbet replied.

The flicker of a smile rested on Doc Gannon's mouth as he regarded her over the rim of his mug.

Lizbet's mind was back on Pearl's illness and all its ramifications. She was just as worried about Ornetta as she was about the woman's granddaughter.

"Pneumonia isn't contagious," she said, and then felt stupid because a person didn't need a medical degree to know that.

Doc Gannon arched one sandy eyebrow. "Correct," he replied.

"Which means there's no danger of anyone else catching it."

"Right again." He looked wry, but still bone-tired, as he raised a forkful of apple cake toward his mouth.

"*Therefore*," Lizbet said pointedly, "I can take Ornetta's place for a while, so she can get some rest."

"You could," the doctor allowed.

"I *will*," Lizbet answered.

"You're quite a woman, Lizbet Fontaine."

"Call me Lizbet, please. And I'm only doing what needs to be done. Ornetta isn't young, you know."

"I've noticed," Doc Gannon allowed. "And if I'm going to call you by your Christian name, you must call me by mine. It's Max."

"I don't think it's proper to address a physician in such a familiar fashion," she responded. She'd already noticed that Doc Gannon didn't wear a wedding band, and she supposed he must be unmarried, since no one had mentioned him having a wife.

He was attractive and easy to talk to, and Lizbet wished she felt the same attraction to him as she did to Gabe Whitfield. Doc Gannon—Max—would have been the more sensible choice.

Not that anybody had asked her to choose.

It was no one's business if she wanted to fantasize a little, now, was it?

"That's up to you, *Miss Fontaine*," came the easy reply.

"All right," Lizbet conceded, spreading her hands for emphasis and nearly overturning her coffee mug. "*All right*, Max."

TWELVE

Since the storm was still raging and the snow was deeper than ever, Gabe didn't attempt to make the arduous journey to the little church at the edge of town for Sunday morning services.

Leaving Hector in the house, much to the dog's displeasure, and keeping a careful grip on the rope he'd strung from there to the barn, Gabe looked after the horses and the cow, checking on them every few hours, and did what he could to keep the chickens happy in their relatively spacious, well-built coop.

When it seemed as if the day would stretch on forever, with nothing to do but wonder when his younger brother would finally put in an appearance, he bundled up, returned to the barn, uncovered the dollhouse he'd been building for Abigail before the bottom fell out of his world, and loaded it onto the old sled he and Finn used to share when they were boys.

It was a difficult task, even with a sled, because the miniature house was good-sized, and Gabe was winded by the time he reentered the kitchen, after struggling to get the thing through the doorway.

Hector, who had been lying in front of the cookstove,

looking forlorn over his recent desertion, got to his feet and gave a curious yip.

"Don't ask what I was thinking," Gabe muttered, then smiled to himself, just realizing how much he talked to the dog. "I don't have an answer."

Maybe his best friend was right; he was alone too much.

He wrestled the bulky toy onto the kitchen table, where it took up most of the space. He'd practically have to hold his plate in his lap when suppertime rolled around.

The dollhouse was in worse shape than he'd anticipated.

Mice had chewed up some of the furniture, and two of the windows, made of real glass and installed with great care, were cracked.

And the whole thing was caked with dirt.

The sight of that dollhouse caused a scalding sensation behind Gabe's eyes. He'd spent months putting it together as a Christmas surprise for his little girl, with lots of help and advice from Bonnie, and somewhere in the house—most likely the attic—there were tiny dolls and dishes and other fittings tucked away in a box.

Over time, Bonnie had collected these and other small items she couldn't make herself, purchasing some from the general store in town, ordering others from Sears, Roebuck and Co.

She'd been as excited about the gift as Abigail would have been, had she lived to see that Christmas.

Choked up, and thoroughly unable to sit still, Gabe left the kitchen, Hector on his heels, crossed the parlor and climbed the stairs.

At the end of the corridor, he lowered the attic steps by pulling the dangling loop of rope marking the spot, and started up.

Almost immediately, he wished he'd brought a lantern; the attic area was gloomy, with shadows clinging to its corners, and he nearly stumbled over Hector, who squirmed past him to explore.

There were trunks aplenty, some going back as far as his parents' younger days, and even his grandparents' time.

He ignored those and, after bracing up, walked over to the place where Bonnie's and Abigail's things were stored.

Abigail's heavy wooden cradle, handmade by Gabe's father, seemed to rock briefly, stirred by an invisible breeze.

He supposed he ought to donate the cradle to someone who needed it, since there weren't likely to be any more babies born on Whitfield farm in the near future.

It was a surprisingly sad concept.

Gabe shoved a hand through his hair and blinked until his vision cleared. There were probably a lot of things going to waste around the place besides the cradle, like the dollhouse and even the old but serviceable sled he'd used to haul it in from the barn.

For the moment, though, he could do nothing.

He hadn't touched either Bonnie's or Abigail's things

since he'd packed them away, with help from John Avery, three years ago.

They would have been constant reminders of his lost wife and child, so he hadn't wanted them in sight. On the other hand, though, he hadn't been able to bring himself to get rid of them.

Now, with his hands shaking a little, he lifted the lid of a beautifully carved chest that had been Bonnie's father's gift to her, when she and Gabe were married.

The scent of her, whispery and faint, rose to greet him, and he squeezed his eyes shut tight against a flood of memories, some sweet, some sorrowful.

Hector nudged his leg and whimpered sympathetically.

Gabe regained his composure, reached out and patted the dog's head reassuringly. "It's all right, boy," he murmured gruffly. "It's all right."

That was a lie, and Hector probably knew that as well as Gabe did.

Bonnie and Abigail were gone, forever.

There was nothing "all right" about that.

He riffled through the clothing and jewelry and embroidered items Bonnie had stored in that trunk, not really looking at any single thing in case it ambushed him and brought him to his knees.

Fortunately, the shoebox where Bonnie had kept the miniatures for Abigail's dollhouse was near the surface.

Gabe tucked it under one arm, carefully lowered the lid of the trunk and turned toward the door.

He and Hector were halfway down the stairs when Gabe heard someone in the kitchen, stomping snow off their boots and then clattering one of the stove lids.

When he reached that part of the house, steeling himself to find Finn there, making himself at home, he found his best friend there instead.

John had hung up his coat and begun adding firewood to the stove. He was a big man, broad in the shoulders, with curly brown hair, now lying wet against his head, and he wore an amused expression, despite the difficulties he must have undergone making his way out from Silver Hills.

"Can't a preacher get a cup of coffee in this place?" he asked, in his jovial, booming voice. Hector was jumping at his feet, wanting a pat on the head.

"The pot's on the stove," Gabe answered, setting aside the shoebox. "There should be some left from breakfast. Help yourself."

John tried to grin and look put-upon at the same time as he bent to ruffle Hector's floppy ears in greeting. "By now, it'll be cold as old Henry Middlebrook's heart, that coffee," he said. "After the ride I just made, I was expecting some hospitality."

Gabe spared his friend a slight smile. "Sit down and I'll

brew some up fresh," he said. "In the meantime, maybe you can tell me what possessed you to risk your life traveling so far in a blinding snowstorm."

John was examining the dollhouse, and his grin faded a little as he probably remembered happier times when Gabe was building it. He'd helped with that, too, forming delicate metal pieces in his blacksmith shop, including a cookstove with a working oven door and even chrome trim.

"You didn't show up for church on Sunday," John said presently, one huge hand gently exploring the shingled roof of the dollhouse. "I figured you stayed home because of the weather, but when you didn't come into town after a couple of days, I decided I'd better come out here and make sure you're still breathing."

"Church wasn't a priority," Gabe answered. "Besides, I don't participate much when I'm there."

"But you still come," John said, grinning again, "and that's what matters."

"Sit down," Gabe said, already pumping water into the coffeepot. He'd be lucky, he reflected, if the pipes didn't freeze. "I'll move the dollhouse someplace else."

John sighed. "This is a fine piece of work, Gabe," he said quietly. "Maybe you ought to forget farming and take up carpentry. Plenty of folks wanting to build new houses and barns and the like, with the war over and all. Country's booming."

Gabe measured ground coffee beans into the pot and set it on the stovetop with a slight bang.

"You been letting Middlebrook bend your ear about me selling him this farm, John?"

John's cheeks reddened, though part of that flush was probably the lingering effects of a long, cold ride out from Silver Hills.

"Henry's a member of my congregation," John said, "and I keep his horses shod, among other things, but we don't talk about much of anything else, Gabe. We especially don't discuss *your* business."

Gabe sighed, got a clean mug down from the shelf to fill for John, once the coffee had come to a boil and then settled a little.

John had remarked, more than once, that Gabe's coffee tasted fine, but it had to be chewed.

Today, though, he just looked at Gabe and waited for what he had coming to him—an apology.

"I know you don't," Gabe admitted, with a long sigh. "I'm sorry."

He started to hoist the dollhouse off the table, so they could set their cups down, anyway, but John stopped him with a brief touch to his arm.

"Leave it," he said. "It's a good sign."

"What's a good sign?" Gabe retorted, testy again, without really knowing why.

"It must have been a job to drag that thing in here from

the barn, and in a near blizzard, no less, and I figure it must have stirred up a lot of hard memories. Still, you did it, and that tells me that you've got a plan. You're fixing to set this dollhouse to rights and give it to some child who'll get some pleasure from it, aren't you?"

"Something like that," Gabe admitted, thoughtful as he considered again that he couldn't give Lizbet's sister a present without providing one for her brother, too. He'd be sure to build something for the boy, too. A toy wagon, maybe, or a sled. That would make it even.

To change the subject, and because he truly wanted to know, he added, "How's Pearl? Did Doc Gannon look in on her?"

Since John boarded at Ornetta's, he'd know.

"She's holding her own," John answered, with a nod and a sigh. "I don't know what Ornetta would do without the newcomer, Lizbet Fontaine. She's been cooking for all of us, and spelling Ornetta by sitting with Pearl, so she can get some rest."

Seated now, John rubbed his beard-stubbled chin thoughtfully and then went on. "She's a good-looking woman, Miss Fontaine. Smart and competent. If I weren't saving every spare cent to bring Mabel out here from Ohio and marry her, I believe I would court her myself."

Gabe bristled at this, even though he had no right, no claim on Lizbet.

"I don't know much about her," he said, as heat began

to surge through the coffeepot on the stove and set it to rattling, metal against metal. He'd wanted to sound casual, nonchalant, but he knew he probably hadn't fooled John.

His friend knew him too well.

Now John's eyes danced with mischief. "That so? I heard you carried her across Main Street the other day, in broad daylight. Whole town's been talking about it."

"I thought you didn't talk about other people's business," Gabe remarked, grabbing the handle of the coffeepot, burning his hand, swearing under his breath and grabbing a pot holder before pouring for each of them.

"I don't," John said, the merriment still in his eyes. "But I'm a preacher, which means I do a whole lot of listening. And the townsfolk, even the ones who've never graced our little church with their presence, seem to have plenty to tell me these days."

"Such as?" Gabe asked, leaning against the counter, coffee cup in hand.

Suddenly, John's expression turned serious. "Such as, she's been looking everywhere for honest work, and good old Henry Middlebrook has put out the word that anybody who hires Lizbet Fontaine will face the consequences of their actions. He wants to marry her—has some kind of devil's bargain with her stepfather."

Gabe nearly dropped his coffee.

It was clear to him now why John had gone to so much trouble to pay him a visit.

"Who told you that?" Gabe asked gruffly.

"It doesn't matter who told me," John answered. "What matters is that Lizbet Fontaine and those two children need help. More help than Ornetta Parkin can give them, bless her soul."

"Henry's stepped over the line this time," Gabe said, and he was dead serious. "Bad enough that he's driven folks off their farms, out of pure greed. Bad enough that he makes life hard for as many people as he can, as often as he can. If he gets away with *this*, it will be over my bloody carcass."

THIRTEEN

By the time the storm ended, five full days after it had begun, Lizbet was exhausted.

She gazed out the window of the room Ornetta and Pearl shared as the previously incessant snow transformed itself into rain, then within mere moments, sleet.

She shivered and pulled her shawl around her in an attempt to stave off the chill.

Not that the house wasn't warm.

There was plenty of firewood, thanks to Gabe Whitfield, and the other boarders kept the kitchen stove and the parlor fireplace roaring.

Pearl's fever had broken at long last, and Max Gannon was sure she'd survive, if she allowed herself the time and rest to recover. She was able to sit up in bed for longer and longer periods, and she took the rich chicken broth Ornetta made for her, though with some reluctance.

Still, the pneumonia had weakened her severely, and she'd been fragile in the first place.

Lizbet, Miss Helen and Miss Ellie took turns sitting with Pearl, reading to her or simply keeping her company, when they could persuade Ornetta to break her vigil for an hour or two to lie down in Lizbet's room or make her way downstairs for coffee or tea or something to eat.

"Miss Lizbet?" Pearl's voice was weak. Hopeful.

Lizbet turned from the window, managed a weary smile. "Just Lizbet," she said softly. "What is it, Pearl? Is there something you need?"

"Is Preacher John back from the blacksmith shop yet?" she asked. "I want him to pray for me."

Lizbet sat down in the chair pulled close to the bed and took Pearl's hand, worried. "I believe he's still working," she said gently. "Are you in pain?"

Pearl's smile was brilliant in her small, childlike face, and she shook her head. "I want him to praise the Lord for me. I ain't got the breath."

Lizbet's eyes stung, and she held Pearl's hand a little tighter. This woman was so innocent, so pure and generous and good that it was a wonder she could even exist in such a difficult world.

Surely, she belonged in a better one.

Though she'd wanted to tell Pearl that she could pray silently, if she wished, and God would surely hear and know she was grateful to be getting well, Lizbet chose to leave those things unsaid.

Instead, she told Pearl that John wouldn't have to be asked to come upstairs and talk with her, hold her hands in that gentle way he had, he with his big self and even bigger heart, because he was sure to appear as soon as he'd returned from his shop, washed up and changed his clothes.

Ever since Pearl had fallen ill, the preacher-blacksmith had visited her every evening but one. The time he was absent, he'd spent the night on Gabe Whitfield's farm, because he'd traveled out there in the storm and been unable to return until the following day.

He'd told Lizbet about this after supper one evening, and since then, he'd seemed to be watching her, not in the troubling way Henry Middlebrook did, but with tender concern. There were things he wanted to say to her, she knew that, but so far he had kept them to himself.

Lizbet had made up her mind to inquire the next time she had a chance to speak to John privately.

"Shall I get you some tea? Maybe some broth?" she asked the patient, having dragged her mind back to the present moment.

Pearl shook her head. "I just want to sleep awhile," she said, and her large, shining eyes drifted closed. Her lids quivered and a smile formed on her lips, as though she were already dreaming.

Lizbet quietly left the room.

When she ventured downstairs, stopping first in the kitchen to make sure Ornetta wasn't there, trying to cook when she should be lying down or just sitting in her favorite chair in the parlor, watching the world pass by on the street, she found John Avery there instead.

Surprised, because it was only two o'clock in the afternoon according to the kitchen clock—she gasped when she saw him.

John, his hands and face pink from a recent scrubbing and a wintery trek back from the blacksmith shop, was standing close to the stove.

He smiled when Lizbet paused on the threshold, struck by the fact that she'd just been thinking of speaking with John and now here he was.

"Good afternoon, Miss Fontaine," he said.

"Lizbet," she corrected him.

"I've been meaning to speak to you," he told her, with a brief nod, hands still extended to absorb the heat from the stove.

It was visible, that warmth, undulating, shifting.

Lizbet sighed, pulled back a chair and sank into it. Frankie and Jubal would be back from school within the hour, wanting to tell her all about their days, and that meant she couldn't let this opportunity for a quiet conversation pass. "That's a coincidence," she replied, "because I've been meaning to speak to you as well."

"Here's our chance," John said affably.

He crossed to the table, took a seat. He was graceful for such a large man, and easygoing. "It's about Henry Middlebrook," he went on, after nearly a full minute of hesitation. "He's been preventing you from getting work,

Miss—er—Lizbet. Telling folks around town that they'd better not hire you."

Lizbet had suspected something like that, since she'd run into a brick wall everywhere she'd gone looking for a job, but she was still infuriated. She felt a hot flush rise, throbbing, from her neck to her face.

"I see," she said, not trusting herself to say more, at least not in that moment. "People are afraid of him, then?"

This time, it was John who sighed. He sounded as tired and overwhelmed as she felt. "Not in the way you're probably thinking. Henry's an old man, and he's not strong, physically at least, but he runs the only bank between here and Painted Pony Creek, Lizbet, and that means he holds a lot of mortgages. Times were hard during the war, and then the epidemic of Spanish flu came along and folks had to borrow against their property, against the next year's crop, against the livestock and equipment they needed. Henry could call in all those loans at any time with one swipe of his pen."

Lizbet felt weak all over, completely defeated. She was nearly out of money, as hard as she'd tried to make her limited funds stretch.

She covered her face with her hands and her shoulders drooped.

John's huge hands grasped her carefully by the wrists and lowered hers, so she would meet his gaze.

"Henry wants to force you to marry him. Am I right?"

Lizbet fought back the threat of tears and barely won the inner skirmish. She could not, *would* not lose her dignity. "I think so."

"Do you know why?"

She shook her head. "Not for sure, but I believe it has something to do with my stepfather, William Keller. William is forever chasing the next business deal, the bigger and riskier it is, the better he likes it. William wants Mr. Middlebrook to invest in his newest venture, whatever it might be, and Mr. Middlebrook apparently wanted *me* in return. As human collateral, if you will. Worse still, I suspect William is planning to use Frankie and Jubal to pressure me into agreeing to the marriage."

"You've heard from your stepfather?" John asked.

"No," Lizbet said. "I don't know what I'll do if I have to give those children back to William. He just up and left them here, you know, without a thought for their welfare. His wife, Marietta, despises them, and I'm afraid they'll be mistreated—or sent to any old boarding school, as long as it's far away, just to get them out of her sight. William will do whatever she wants him to, he's so besotted with the woman."

"Quite a story," John said with another sigh, this time one of regret. "Isn't it possible that Mr. Keller left his children behind simply because he and his wife wanted to be rid of them? Doesn't he have any kind of fatherly love for them?"

Tears sprang to Lizbet's eyes then, and she couldn't stop them from slipping, stinging, down her cheeks, which were chapped from her forays to the general store and the schoolhouse and to various businesses, seeking employment in the cold weather. Miss Helen walked the children to school in the mornings, but Lizbet sometimes went to meet them in the afternoons, as eager to see them again as if they'd just returned from the other side of the world.

"I don't know what to do," she confessed. "I've prayed and prayed, in church and out, and no solution has come to me, either for keeping Frankie and Jubal with me or for finding work. I wonder sometimes if God is listening."

John smiled. "He's listening," he assured her. "But God works through people most of the time, and I reckon right about now, He wants me to help out however I can."

Lizbet laughed through her tears. "I'm sorry," she said, wiping her eyes and cheeks with the sleeve of her practical brown woolen dress. "I'm no blacksmith."

At that, John laughed, too. "I wasn't talking about hiring you to work the forge, Lizbet, or pound horseshoes into shape with a steel mallet. But I do have something in mind—something I can't mention just yet because I need to discuss it with someone else first—but even if it happens, it would only solve half your problem."

Hope surged through Lizbet's brave, bruised heart. "Is it a way to keep the children?" she asked, almost breathless.

John sighed and shook his head regretfully. "That still needs some figuring out," he answered. "I do know a good lawyer over in Painted Pony Creek. Name's Tom Hollister. He might be able to help, since Mr. Keller basically abandoned those little ones—in your care, it's true, but it's still a callous thing to do. Did he give you any money for their keep, Lizbet?"

"No," Lizbet answered, saddened again. She couldn't afford to pay a lawyer. Once the money stitched into the hem of her fancy coat had been used up, she would be destitute. "No, he didn't give me money."

"That's another point in your favor," John commented. "But let's worry about it later."

"I never *stop* worrying," Lizbet said truthfully. "I can't lose my sister and brother, John. Not to anybody." Here, her voice broke. "I love them so much, and I promised our mother I would make sure they are well cared for, no matter what."

He didn't respond to her statement directly.

"You come to church every Sunday," John replied good-naturedly. "Haven't you been listening to my sermons? Faith and worry don't go together. You've got to trust God to help you get through this, Lizbet. There *will* be a solution."

"But you're not going to tell me what your idea is? For finding work, I mean?"

John's smile was warm. "No," he replied succinctly.

With that, he pushed back his chair, rose to his feet and headed upstairs, most likely to sit with Pearl.

Lizbet waited several minutes, then retreated to the attic room, where she riffled through her trunks until she found the special coat she'd once worn to operas and symphony concerts.

The rent was due soon, although Ornetta had offered to let it pass this month, out of gratitude for Lizbet's help with Pearl and many of the household tasks. Trouble was, Ornetta couldn't be expected to do that for everyone, and all of the boarders had assisted, one way or another.

So Lizbet had politely refused.

Now she sat down on the edge of the bed she still shared with both the children, the lovely, frivolous coat in her lap, and turned it inside out to get to the spot in the hem where the last of her personal savings was hidden.

In the next moment, a terrible shock barreled into her like some great beast on a dead run, and shook her to her soul.

The special place in the hem was already undone, and the money was gone.

FOURTEEN

༄

The discovery bent Lizbet double, and she could barely catch her breath. The money she'd so carefully hidden in the hem of her velvet coat was *gone*.

She'd stitched those folded bills carefully out of sight, and it wasn't as if they could have fallen out.

No, someone had deliberately opened the stitches and stolen them.

Lizbet didn't need to ask herself who that someone was, because she knew.

Marietta.

Somehow, William's insatiable wife had found Lizbet's hiding place, even though Lizbet had made every effort to keep the money a secret from everyone, including Frankie and Jubal and certainly William.

Had Marietta suspected, and searched through Lizbet's private things when she was occupied elsewhere, with the children for instance? The journey out from St. Louis had been long and arduous, and the task of looking after Frankie and Jubal had definitely fallen to Lizbet.

Before they all left St. Louis, traveling most of the way West by railroad, Marietta hadn't had access to Lizbet's belongings, at least not *easy* access.

Except when they stopped to rest for a day or two along the way, which happened twice, much to William's impatience, the bulk of Lizbet's baggage had been safely locked away, in the care of porters and the like.

It didn't matter when or how it had happened, Lizbet decided.

Except for a few dollar bills still pinned to the inside of her bodice, there was no money to meet even their simplest needs.

Quietly frantic, she began to search through those things she had yet to unpack.

But nothing else was missing.

Her mother's delicate heirloom ruby necklace was still in its worn velvet case, along with a single strand of pearls that had belonged to Lizbet's maternal grandmother.

The remainder of the jewelry was of the costume variety, mostly gifts from her friends, her mother and her favorite and long-dead Aunt Dora. Lizbet preferred to dress simply and rarely wore baubles of any kind.

It was, of course, conceivable that a railroad or hotel employee had found Lizbet's carefully hidden bills and coins, but how would they have known where to look for it? And why, if one or more of them were thieves, hadn't they taken any of her jewelry, especially the two valuable pieces?

No, she'd been right in the beginning.

Marietta had found, and stolen, practically every penny

Lizbet had or was likely to have, given the way her job search was going.

Hardly able to hold back sobs of frustration and rage and sheer helplessness, Lizbet buried her face in the soft velvet of her only truly fancy garment and breathed, just breathed, slowly and deeply.

"Lizbet?"

The voice was small, tentative. Full of concern.

Frankie.

"What's wrong?" the child asked, standing in the doorway.

Lizbet had heard neither her approach nor her entry, and she instantly straightened her spine and lifted her chin and did her level best to smile at her sister.

"Nothing," Lizbet lied. She abhorred liars, but there was no point in making the children bear *her* burdens.

"I don't believe you," Frankie replied. "You're just being strong so me and Jubal won't be scared."

"Jubal and I," Lizbet corrected automatically.

Frankie rolled her eyes. "Jubal and *I*, then," she replied, after several moments spent studying her older sister. "I still don't believe you. Something's happened. Is it Father? Is he back in Silver Hills?"

Lizbet shook her head, set the coat aside and practically leaped to her feet, hurrying across the small room to hug Frankie. "Your father isn't here," she assured the child. "Not yet, anyway."

"You think he'll come and take Jubal and me—Jubal and *I*?—away to live with him and that dreadful Marietta, don't you?"

There was no sense, Lizbet realized, in trying to fool Frankie; she was too smart, and getting smarter with every passing day.

"Yes," she admitted reluctantly. "Yes, Frankie, I do worry about that."

"Marietta doesn't want us," Frankie said, with a stalwart certainty that made Lizbet's heart crumble. "You know she doesn't, Lizbet. And Father's willing to make a fool of himself over her—that's obvious." She paused. "He's like an organ-grinder's monkey, dancing and tumbling and rolling around on the ground."

As grave as their present situation was, Lizbet had to smile at her sister's imagination and the picture it brought to mind of a miniature, furry William, wearing a red velvet vest and a gold-trimmed fez to match, performing for Marietta's amusement and, yes, any coins that might be tossed his way.

Hers was a broken smile, though, and it fell away almost immediately because despite her antipathy toward her stepfather—*former* stepfather, she supposed, now that he was married to Marietta instead of her mother—Lizbet knew William was being used and, though subtly, humiliated.

And she wouldn't have wished that on anyone—not even Henry Middlebrook.

She centered her attention on Frankie again.

The skirt of the little girl's calico dress was speckled with mud, and she was in her stocking feet. Since she wasn't wearing her coat, hat and boots, she must have been home from school for a while.

"Where's Jubal?" Lizbet asked, instantly worried. Frankie was three years older than Jubal and growing up fast, but they were still nearly inseparable, especially when they weren't with their elder sister.

"He's in the kitchen," Frankie answered, with a note of affectionate disdain. "Ornetta's making cherry pies to go with supper, and he says he wants to help."

With that, Frankie crossed the room, found a clean dress to wear, and turned her back so Lizbet could undo the buttons of the one she had on.

The last warm and sunny day had been in mid-October, and Lizbet had leaped at the chance to do her family's laundry, as well as her own. From now on through to spring, any garment she washed would have to be hung up on the folding rack Ornetta kept in the kitchen for just such times.

She'd considered taking in washing and ironing to make money, but most people around Silver Hills handled such ordinary, if arduous, tasks themselves, just as they raised gardens and kept chickens and cattle to feed their families.

She sighed again, briefly wondered what John Avery's

plan was and when he would get around to telling her about it, then left Frankie lacing up dry shoes and headed down the rear stairway.

"Ornetta Parkin," she scolded gently, watching as the older woman placed two pies carefully inside the oven on the wood cookstove, "you're supposed to be taking it easy. You'll exhaust yourself."

Ornetta smiled in mock defiance. She jutted out her chin, too, but her eyes sparkled with kindly glee.

"I appreciate all you've done to help me and Pearl these past days, Lizbet, and don't you ever think I don't." Here, Jubal, seated at the table, glanced his sister's way, probably wondering if she was about to correct Ornetta's grammar, the way she did his and Frankie's. "Just the same, this is my boarding house and it's my job to look after the people who live here. And I dare say, I make the best cherry pie in the State of Montana."

Just being in Ornetta's presence, now that she was essentially her old self again, or mostly so, cheered Lizbet immeasurably.

"I won't argue with that," she said with a smile, ruffling Jubal's already-mussed blond hair as she passed him.

"You just ask Gabe Whitfield if you don't believe me," Ornetta went on, as though Lizbet hadn't spoken.

At the mention of Gabe, Lizbet's spirits dipped a little. He'd been to the boarding house just once since that first visit, delivering a second load of wood for Ornetta's stove and fireplace, but he hadn't brought Hector along and he hadn't come inside for pie and coffee, like before.

The disappointment Lizbet had felt, unjustified though it was, was with her still.

"I saw Gabe going into the general store a little while ago," Ornetta went on, shutting the heavy oven door and placing her hands on the small of her back as she turned away from the stove. "I sent a neighbor boy over to invite him to supper tonight, and he sent word back that he'd come, on account of my cherry pie."

Lizbet felt a flutter in her midsection, not entirely unpleasant, and pressed one hand to the base of her throat, where her heartbeat was suddenly pounding away like a jungle drum.

Ornetta chuckled. "You're taken with that man," she told Lizbet. "I thought so. I surely did."

Jubal spoke up. "If Lizbet is taken, me and Frankie are going, too."

Lizbet realized she was too tired to correct the boy, though it felt like dereliction of duty. Was she forgetting how to teach?

"That's not what is meant here," Ornetta explained kindly, seating herself at the table with a heavy sigh and reaching over to pat Jubal on top of the head. "Would you please do me a favor, young Mr. Jubal Keller, and run on in to the parlor to see if the ladies are home yet? I reckon they could do with some tea and a few cookies, if they are."

Jubal was on his feet instantly, looking as vigilant as a little soldier. "Cookies?" he echoed. "There are *cookies*?"

Ornetta laughed, and it was a joyful sound, one that soothed Lizbet's heart, because it reminded her that there was, problems notwithstanding, a lot of good in the world. "Indeed there are, young man. I made them while you and your sister were at school, and I reckon I can spare a few, provided you do what I asked you to."

Jubal raced out of the kitchen, lively obedience personified.

"How much do you know about Gabe Whitfield?" Ornetta asked, the moment he'd gone. The change in her countenance was marked.

Lizbet shrugged, trying to sound casual. "Not very much," she conceded. "He's a widower—he owns a farm—he and John Avery have been friends since they were in the Army together. That's about all."

"John tell you anything more than that?"

Lizbet shook her head.

Jubal burst into the kitchen again, like a cannonball breaching a stone wall. "They're home! All the ladies and Mr. Ernshaw, too. And they *all* want cookies and tea."

"Well, now, that's fine," Ornetta said, in the same affable tone she'd used before. "I'll put the kettle on, and you can take a plate of cookies upstairs for you and your sister to share." Frankie often stayed in the attic room after school, reading or working on her lessons until supper.

Jubal was thrilled to be the bearer of Ornetta's baked goods.

The innocent ability to find delight in simple pleasures. When had she, Lizbet, lost that?

Smiling fondly, Ornetta placed six good-sized oatmeal and raison cookies on a plate and handed the plate to the little boy.

"*Share*," Lizbet reminded her brother, as he started up the rear stairway, yelling, "Frankie! I've got cookies!"

Hearing him clattering along the upstairs corridor to the steps leading to their shared room, Lizbet shook her head ruefully.

"I'll speak to him—again—about running in the house," she told Ornetta. "He knows Pearl needs to rest a lot, but he forgets. Especially when cookies are part of the equation."

Ornetta filled the teakettle, but it was Lizbet who began preparing a tray for the other boarders warming up by the parlor fire.

The older woman picked up their earlier conversation right where she'd left off. "I was fixing to tell you about Gabe. He's had it hard. He was shot in the leg while he was training with the Army, and now he's got that limp. If that wasn't enough, well, both his parents drowned crossing the Flathead River when he was still a young bridegroom and about to be a father himself. Then, like I told you, the Spanish influenza came along, and Gabe lost his wife, Bonnie, and their little girl, Abigail. It was just awful, I'm telling you. If John Avery and just about everybody else in this community hadn't stood by him the way they did, I'm not sure he would have bothered to go on living."

Lizbet could well imagine the town rallying, with few exceptions, around a young man nearly broken under the weight of his grief. Especially Ornetta and John.

What would it be like to truly belong in a town like Silver Hills, Montana?

Lizbet longed to know.

But first, she needed work. More desperately than ever.

So, without a word of explanation to anyone, Ornetta included, she put on her coat, marched through the front room without looking either to the left or to the right and left the house.

The street was quiet now that evening was approaching, but Lizbet well knew that Henry Middlebrook was still inside the bank building; he was well-known for working late.

And she wanted a word with him.

By the time she'd crossed the street and walked the two blocks to his establishment, she'd worked herself up into a state of high dudgeon.

She stood before the double glass doors for a few

moments, then pushed them open with the palms of both hands and stormed inside.

A few customers lingered and, evidently sensing Lizbet's confrontational attitude, they finished their business quickly and withdrew.

"The bank is *closed*," Henry told her, rounding the counter.

"I didn't come here to do any banking," Lizbet replied coldly. "I'm here to tell you that I know what you've been doing—undermining my efforts to find honest work—and I *will not tolerate this mistreatment another day!*"

Middlebrook arched his bushy gray eyebrows. "Is that so? And how do you propose to stop me?"

So, he wasn't denying his reprehensible behavior. It was probably the closest he'd ever come to honesty.

"If necessary, I will stand up in the next town meeting and tell everyone what you've been doing!"

At that, he actually laughed.

It required all Lizbet's restraint not to slap his fat, smug face with all her strength. And for a moment, she was stuck for an answer.

"All your problems could be solved so easily, Elizabeth. So simply. Finding work would be unnecessary." He paused and leaned in a little, and his nasty breath struck her face. "All you need to do is marry me, and you will have everything you could possibly want. You could live in a mansion, instead of the attic of a boarding house."

"I would sooner die than marry a pompous, hypocritical snake like you!" Lizbet said angrily. "And *do not* address me by my first name. In fact, do not address me at all. Ever!"

Suddenly Henry Middlebrook was offended, not amused. But, perhaps stunned by Lizbet's forthright statement, he didn't offer a reply.

Feeling better for having spoken her mind, even though nothing had really changed, Lizbet turned and walked out onto the snowy sidewalk, warmed through and through by her own anger.

A farmer she recognized from church stepped up beside her, touched her elbow lightly and briefly.

"Good for you, Miss," he said. "Except for John Avery and Gabe Whitfield, I've never seen anybody stand up to that old man quite like you did."

Lizbet smiled. "Thank you," she replied.

And then she headed back toward the boarding house.

Supper must be almost ready, and Gabe would be there soon to share the meal.

For the moment, she forgot all about Henry Middlebrook and his mean-spirited lechery—her mind was on Gabe Whitfield.

FIFTEEN

༄

Gabe loved having supper in Ornetta's kitchen; it was warm and fragrant with good things that night—corned beef hash, green beans and biscuits and the promised cherry pie.

She had invited him often, but he'd mostly refused, not wanting to inflict his gloomy disposition on someone who had never forgotten how to laugh, how to hope, how to love.

Tonight he hadn't been able to resist. Hadn't wanted to go home to an empty house, where there would be no one there to greet him except the dog, and the fire in the cookstove would have gone out, leaving the whole place chilly.

Hector was fine; he had water and food and a fur coat. Fine, too, were the cow, the chickens and the remaining horse, Abednego; they all had what they needed.

He'd ridden into town around noon, meaning to buy a few supplies, things he could carry in his saddlebags, then return home and work on repairing the dollhouse, and when the boy Ornetta sent to tell him he ought to come to supper found him in the general store, he'd ruffled the lad's hair, given him a nickel and sent him straight back to say thanks, he'd be there for sure.

Gabe had spent the intervening hours at the blacksmith's shop, helping John repair wagon wheels and the like.

In between working the forge and hammering away at pieces of molten iron, they'd talked, and by the time they arrived at Ornetta's place, they were both tired, covered in soot and strangely hopeful.

At least, Gabe was hopeful, because his friend had given him an idea. John, meanwhile, looked about as smug as a good man could without committing the sin of pride.

And sin was something John avoided at all possible costs.

Once both men had washed up, trying not to leave a mess in the process, most of the boarders, including the children, had been served their evening meal in the dining room and then retreated to the front parlor or their private quarters.

Frankie and Jubal, disappointed that Hector hadn't come to town with Gabe, went to bed without protest.

John had told him, while explaining the plan he proposed, that both children and Lizbet shared a narrow bed in the room Pearl had kindly vacated to make room for them.

This, along with the things John had spoken of during his visit to the farmhouse that stormy night, concerning Henry's schemes, troubled him greatly.

A separate table had been set in the kitchen, with places for John, Ornetta, Lizbet and himself, and the result was a rare sensation of being encompassed in comfort and well-being.

Gabe felt at home in a way he seldom did these days, and he knew it wasn't because of the place, but because of the people gathered there for a friendly supper.

Everyone seemed to be in a jovial mood—except Lizbet.

She'd greeted Gabe cordially enough, but she was weary and defeated. He saw that right away, though she certainly tried to hide her low spirits.

There was a flush in her cheeks that seemed more indicative of fever than anything else.

Given all he'd learned from John, both today at the blacksmith's shop and on the night the blizzard had peaked, when they'd stayed in the kitchen well into the small hours, swilling strong coffee, playing poker for matchsticks and doing more talking than Gabe had done in the last three years put together, he knew what was troubling Lizbet.

She was in a spot, just as John had said earlier that day, and as things stood, he, Gabe Whitfield, was the only person around who could help her in a real and lasting way. And, as John had also pointed out, he stood to benefit from the plan as well.

And so it was that, after supper, when John and Ornetta made a show of being too worn out to do more than fall into their beds for a good night's sleep, Gabe and Lizbet were left to clear the table and wash the dishes by themselves.

Lizbet didn't protest, though Gabe suspected she was barely able to stay on her feet. She filled the sink with hot water from the copper boiler John had long since installed above it, along with two others in the bathing rooms, while Gabe gathered and scraped plates into an empty lard tin for Hector to enjoy later.

Gabe was not good at starting conversations—even with Bonnie, he had rarely had to do that, since she always had so much to say—but that night he made the effort.

"John told me about the situation you're in," Gabe said to Lizbet's back, as she added soap to the hot dishwater. "And I think I can help."

She stiffened, turned her head to look at him over her right shoulder. "I don't understand," she said, and dear God, she sounded so beaten down that he wanted to take her into his arms and hold her until she'd cried out all the tears she'd probably been holding back for years.

He didn't, though, because that would have sent entirely the wrong message. Not the one he felt ready to send, at least.

Lizbet turned, drying her hands on the apron she'd put on as soon as supper was over. "What did you mean, Mr. Whitfield?" she asked, straightening her shoulders and lifting her chin. "How can you help?"

Tendrils of her glorious red-gold hair curled around her face, damp from the steam rising from the sink and the heat surging from the stove.

Gabe didn't bother to correct her, insist that she call him by his first name. It wasn't the right time for that, either.

She was understandably wary, and knowing that tied Gabe's tongue in a knot. Took him a full minute to untangle it, and by that time, he was red in the face.

"I'm a widower," he finally managed to say. "My wife and daughter have been gone for over three years now."

Lizbet's countenance softened visibly. "I know," she said, almost in a whisper. "I'm so sorry."

At that, Gabe's eyes burned and his throat tightened, so he nodded, swallowed hard and prayed for the grace to speak like a sensible man instead of falling apart.

"How can you help me?" she asked, and now tears filled her eyes.

Gabe took a step toward her, bound and determined to kiss her, but he stopped himself in time, God be thanked.

"My house is big and it's empty, except for Hector and me," he heard himself say, as if from a small distance. "I've got my hands full, most of the year, raising crops and looking after the livestock, and that means I never get around to cleaning the place properly. Most it gets is a spit and a lick, and then Hector and I are off to the barn or the fields or into the hills to cut wood."

Lizbet waited, though Gabe thought he saw the faintest glow of light gathering in her beautiful green eyes. Under their sheen of tears, they shone like polished emeralds.

"What I'm trying to get said here, Miss Fontaine, is

that I need some help around the place—cleaning, cooking, mending and the like. Doing the wash, too, when the weather allows. I know that's a lot of work, and that you're a teacher, not a housemaid, but I can pay you a reasonable wage, and since there's plenty of room in the place, you and the children can all have your own rooms."

Lizbet opened her mouth, closed it again. Her hands twisted the skirt of her apron as though to wring it out after washing.

Gabe was compelled to rush on, though it felt as though he were running and stumbling down a steep slope, barely able to keep from losing his balance and going head over heels to land at the bottom in a quivering heap.

"I want you to know that I don't expect any more from you than keeping house," he said, and then blushed so hard that his face actually burned. "Laundry and ironing, too, I guess," he added, willing himself to shut up.

He should have let John make the initial proposal. He was a preacher, self-appointed or not.

John knew how to say things in a way that made sense.

"You're offering me honest work and a place for Frankie and Jubal and me to live," Lizbet said, feeling her way through that sentence the way she might feel her way across a rickety footbridge in the dark of night.

"Yes." One word. But he got that right, anyway. Inside him, a strange combination of joy and wariness sparked and caught fire.

Dear God, he thought, *don't let her refuse.*

"I will not be sharing your bed, Mr. Whitfield," she said pointedly, lifting her chin and squaring her shoulders.

More's the pity, Gabe thought, but what he said was, "Absolutely not. You have nothing to fear from me, Miss Fontaine. I still love my wife, and I always will."

She flinched slightly, as though he'd delivered a blow, albeit a light one, and raised her chin again. "Then we have an agreement," she said formally, "though I'm not sure I can start right away, since Pearl is laid up and Ornetta needs my help."

Gabe nodded, thrilled and doing his damnedest not to show it. Plus, he admired her loyalty, though saying so would probably have been too much. He didn't want to sound obsequious or anything like that.

"That's fine," he said instead. "Whenever you're ready and the roads are clear enough to travel by wagon, I'll come for you and the children and all your belongings."

Just then, a change came over her.

Lizbet seemed to lose the starch in her knees, for she took a stumbling step forward and gripped the back of a chair to steady herself.

Gabe was beside her immediately, taking a gentle hold on her arm, lest she slip to the floor. "Sit down," he said, pulling out the chair and pressing her into it.

She began to weep, even to sob, however softly, into the palms of her hands. Her shoulders trembled, and Gabe felt as helpless as a mouse in a cage full of tigers.

He went to the sink to fill a glass of water, but the boiler was going, so it came out hot.

"What is it?" he asked, alarmed.

She sniffled. Shook her head, as though to shake away her tears.

And finally spoke. "I'm so relieved," she blurted. "I told Henry Middlebrook what I thought of him today, and I felt good about it, until I remembered that I was still broke with no sign of finding a job." Lizbet paused here, and drew in a shaky breath. "Now I finally have, and there's not a thing he can do about it."

Gabe grinned. "Not a thing," he confirmed.

By then, she was sitting up straight in her chair, having recovered her dignity.

Gabe returned to the table, sat down next to her and dared to take her hand. "All right, then," he told her. "We have an agreement."

In the next instant, he regretted holding Lizbet's hand. He'd just told her, for pity's sake, that she needn't fear forward behavior from him. He flushed, went to let go and felt her fingers tighten briefly around his.

She sniffled again, nodded. "Yes," she said. "We have an agreement. And I thank you kindly for it. Not only for offering me the work I need so badly, but for not treating me as a commodity, to be bought, sold or traded."

Gabe didn't need to ask what she meant by that last part. She was referring to the alleged "deal" between her stepfather and Henry Middlebrook.

And the thought brought his blood to a steady boil.

SIXTEEN

Two weeks before Christmas, there was a thaw in the weather, melting away much of the snow, soon followed by a hard freeze, which made the roads perilous, if still passable.

Because Pearl's health had greatly improved, and both Nelly Carlyle and Stella MacIntosh were helping out with the cooking and housework in their spare time, Ornetta was well rested and almost ready to resume her usual schedule.

All of this meant that Lizbet could, in good conscience, leave the boarding house with Frankie and Jubal and take up her new position as Gabe Whitfield's housekeeper.

The relief of being able to provide for herself and her siblings in an honorable way was tremendous, and she found herself humming happily as she packed the few belongings that had been taken from their trunks and valises upon arriving at Ornetta's.

One fine December morning, Gabe arrived, as previously agreed, driving his buckboard. This time, Hector accompanied him.

John had taken the day off from blacksmithing, and he and Gabe carried everything Lizbet and the children owned downstairs and out to the wagon, where they loaded the bulky objects carefully and covered them with a tarp.

It had been nearly a full month since Gabe had offered Lizbet work, and she had accepted, which meant that practically everyone in town knew.

Lizbet was not so naive as to think there wasn't gossip about her and Gabe, but she couldn't afford to dwell on it.

Silver Hills was a good town, but every place had busybodies, folks with so little of interest in their own lives that they groped and grabbed for it in the lives of others.

Just two Sundays ago, in fact, a woman named Susan Henderson had stood up in the middle of that week's church service to announce in a ringing voice of righteous indignation that Lizbet Fontaine and Gabe Whitfield were about to commence living in sin, right under all their noses.

A hubbub had arisen, followed by John Avery's midsermon intervention. He had cleared his throat loudly, leveled his gaze at the troublemaker and told her to go outside and fetch a stone.

She, along with the rest of the congregation, including Gabe and Lizbet, who weren't even sitting together, stared at him in confusion.

John swept up everyone present—man, woman and child—in a single sweeping glance. "If any of you agree with Miss Henderson here, then you'd best go out and find yourself a stone, too." He paused, and Lizbet, despite her red-faced mortification, had thought he would cut an impressive figure on any stage in the world.

No one had moved except the reprimanded, who dropped back into her seat on the pew as if she'd been struck in the forehead by a pebble from a slingshot.

John had scanned them again, his expression grim. "No takers?" he'd inquired solemnly, his usually gentle eyes hot with a fury fit for the prophets of old. In those moments, he might as well have been Isaiah himself, or Elijah, such power did he exude. "No one here is without sin and thus qualified to throw the first stone?" he'd demanded, in a voice like a thin sheet of metal rippling in a hurricane wind.

No one had spoken.

And no one had gone to fetch a stone.

Remembering that incident as John and Gabe stood somewhat awkwardly in Ornetta's parlor, waiting for Lizbet to say her goodbyes, Lizbet silently reminded herself that as long as her own conscience was clear, it didn't matter one whit what others thought. Or said.

The way Ornetta and Lizbet clung to each other, their eyes brimming with tears, a person would have thought they were about to be parted forever, which, of course, they weren't. The bond between the two of them, Lizbet knew, would hold forever, but saying goodbye and leaving the warm friendliness of that house was beyond difficult, just the same.

Frankie and Jubal, bundled up against the cold, were ready to move in and share a house with their beloved friend, Hector. They'd already bid a solemn farewell to everyone in the boarding house, and Pearl had baked and packed two dozen sugar cookies to sustain them on their five-mile journey to the Whitfield farm.

So they shifted impatiently from one foot to the other, in amusing tandem, while their elder sister turned to embrace Pearl, being careful not to hold her too tightly, for though she had recovered, she was still delicate.

Blessedly, the other boarders were out of the house, though each one had taken time, the evening before, to wish Lizbet and the children every good fortune.

Presently, the ceremony of parting was concluded, and John led the children and Hector toward his own wagon, which stood behind Gabe's under the clear, ice-blue sky, and helped them scramble their way into it.

As there was no room for them in Gabe's wagon, Frankie was to ride with John, on the seat, a dignified little soul in her layers of wool clothing, while Jubal, similarly clad, settled in the back, with an exuberant Hector to keep him company.

Lizbet, it had been tacitly decided, was to join Gabe on the high seat of his buckboard, and she did. He'd brought heavy blankets to cover her lap and legs, and she was feeling grateful and unaccountably shy in the bargain.

She knew townspeople were watching, some kindly,

raising a friendly hand to acknowledge the little convoy, while others peered out from behind curtains, Lizbet was sure, clucking in disapproval and shaking their heads at this example of what the world was coming to.

She smiled and waved back to the good people coming in and out of the general store and the saloon and the other establishments along Main Street. For the benefit of the disdainful ones, she kept her shoulders straight and her chin high.

Deep down, where no one but God could see, she actually felt a little thrill at the prospect of living—chastely, of course—under the same roof as Gabe Whitfield.

The ride to the farm was long, cold and, although Lizbet would have preferred it otherwise, almost entirely silent, at least in Gabe's wagon. Laughter and merriment rang through the sharp chill of the December air from the one carrying John, the children and Hector.

Gabe's mood was pensive, and that caused Lizbet to wonder, after several minutes, if he was regretting his decision to open his undoubtedly quiet home to her and two lively children. He hadn't reacted at all, as far as Lizbet knew, to that Sunday of prospective stone throwing, except to set his jaw and glare at the flush-faced miscreant.

He'd told Lizbet straight out, that night in Ornetta's kitchen when he'd offered her employment, that he still loved his wife.

In other words, her virtue was safe with him.

That was reassuring but, strangely, it had caused something within Lizbet to sink a little, and so far it had never resurfaced, whatever *it* was. Hope? The first, faint glimmer of love?

Lizbet did *not* love Gabe Whitfield, she reminded herself, as they jostled along over slippery roads, frozen solid.

But she *could*. Oh, yes. She definitely could come to love him. Would probably never love any man *except* him.

Why was she so sure of that?

Because Gabe was everything she believed a man should be—honorable, strong, hardworking, smart, generous. And a thousand other things she couldn't yet name, but merely sensed whenever he was near.

She had never met another man like him except, perhaps, her late father, whom she had admired as well as adored.

Gabe, unlike her father and John Avery, his most valued friend, was a man who kept to himself for the most part, which made it all the more surprising that he'd set this potentially scandalous plan in motion to start with.

Was he regretting it now that the big day had actually arrived?

Lizbet found that prospect hard to bear, and for all her self-discipline, she wasn't able to stay silent.

"Mr. Whitfield?"

He turned his head, looked down into her face. His own was red with cold, but with an odd glow underneath, and though his mouth didn't smile, his gray eyes did. "Yes, Miss Fontaine?" he asked, with pointed formality.

"Are you sorry?"

"For what?"

Lizbet fidgeted on the hard seat of the buckboard and fiddled with the blankets in her lap, wishing she hadn't spoken up after all. Now there was nothing to do but follow through with her real question.

"Are you sorry you gave me a job? That Frankie and Jubal and I are moving into your house? We might be a disruption—"

At last, he smiled. *Really* smiled, in a way Lizbet had never seen him do before. "I'm not," he said, with cheerful resolution. "Are you sorry you agreed?"

Lizbet shook her head, so earnest in her answer that she couldn't wait to say *no* aloud.

"I'm—we're very grateful for the opportunity," she said moments later.

They were rounding a corner, and when they'd made the turn, Lizbet was heartened to see that the road leading to the house was lined by cottonwoods. Bare-branched in the cold of winter, like sketches against a painfully blue sky, in spring and summer and even into fall, they would be covered in glittering leaves.

"You might change your mind," Gabe replied in a wry tone, "when you find out how much work it'll be, keeping up a farmhouse the size of mine."

"I won't at all," Lizbet said, thinking of the simple luxuries that awaited her, like a bed of her own and worthwhile tasks to occupy her time every day. Except for the prospect of William taking Frankie and Jubal from her, or Mr. Middlebrook pulling some dastardly trick out of his hat, she had no worries at all. "You'll find that I am a diligent worker, Mr. Whitfield, well worth my wages."

"I'm sure you will be," Gabe replied quietly. "But if you change your mind and decide to take up another profession elsewhere, I won't give you any trouble over it. If you stay, it will be difficult at times, especially if my brother, Finn, shows up, which he's promised to do."

Lizbet stared at him, eyebrows lifted. This was the first she'd heard of his having a brother, though John might have mentioned it during one of their conversations.

"Is he so troublesome?" she asked. "Your brother, I mean?"

Gabe shook his dark head, resettled his hat with a motion of one hand, and he looked more amused than irritated. "I wouldn't say that. Finn's a good man, but he's one of those types who take up more space and use up more air than other people."

Lizbet was left to ponder the meaning of that cryptic reply.

SEVENTEEN

༼ཉ༽

The house itself seemed to welcome Lizbet and the children; Gabe could have sworn it expanded, as though taking a deep breath, as if to make room for them.

If he hadn't known better—he was not a man given to whimsical ideas—he would have said the place had been as lonely as he had, every bit as full of shadows and the vast emptiness of grief.

Complete foolishness, he concluded.

John, good friend that he was, had undertaken the task of unhitching Shadrach and Abednego from Gabe's wagon and turning them out in the pasture to "soak up some sunshine while it's here," as he put it.

Gabe appreciated the time to show Lizbet the house and, at the same time, wished John was there to act as a buffer between this vibrantly lovely woman and whatever it was he felt toward her. He worried that he might reveal something about his feelings that he had yet to understand himself.

Frankie and Jubal, after pausing near the kitchen stove to let Lizbet unbundle them from their many items of extra clothing, looked awestruck.

"This here is the biggest kitchen I've ever been in,"

Jubal piped up, his blue eyes wide. "Can we look around the whole place, Mr. Whitfield? Please?"

Out of the corner of his eye, Gabe saw Lizbet open her mouth, probably to protest such eager audacity or perhaps correct the boy's grammar, then close it again, though reluctantly.

Inwardly, Gabe smiled.

"Go ahead," he said, then paused and glanced at Lizbet. "If it's all right with your sister, that is."

Lizbet sighed, but softly and with benevolent disapproval. "Mind your manners, and don't go looking behind closed doors."

"What if *all* the doors are closed?" Jubal wanted to know.

"Then I guess you'll have to content yourselves with keeping to the corridors."

"I'll watch him," Frankie promised, standing just behind Jubal and laying a gentle but still restraining hand on his small shoulder.

Lizbet merely nodded at that, and before anyone could say another word, Jubal bolted toward the door leading to the large, modestly furnished parlor and banged his way past it.

Frankie went after him, and so did Hector, but the little dickens was fast, and moments later, both Gabe and Lizbet could hear his boot soles pounding their way across the plank floor and then up the stairs. Unlike many good-sized houses of the day, Gabe's did not have a rear stairway leading up from the kitchen.

Lizbet closed her eyes and pressed the fingertips of one hand to her temple. "I'm sorry," she said, with a little moan that landed in Gabe's middle like a spark. "Our room at Ornetta's was cramped, and I guess Jubal was bound to feel the need to bust out as soon as there was space to do it."

"Don't worry," Gabe answered, grateful that the conversation was so simple and ordinary. The thoughts and images whirling around in his head at the moment were anything but, and that spark in his belly was burning hotter and sinking lower at the same time.

He moved to the stove to build up the fire, recalling too late that he should have helped Lizbet—*Miss Fontaine*—out of her coat, as any gentleman would have done.

"John will expect some hot coffee when he comes in," he said, and then felt like an even bigger fool than before. To cover his embarrassment, he clattered stove lids about and made a grand hoopla rinsing out and filling the blue enamel coffeepot.

During that enterprise, Lizbet divested herself of the heavy and somewhat threadbare weight of the garment, along with her knitted gloves, which she stuffed into one of the pockets. Then she hung the coat from one of the wall hooks next to the back door, alongside Gabe's own and those of her brother and sister.

With a barely suppressed smile, inspired by the clatter

of two laughing children and one dog running happily from one end of the upstairs hallway to the other, by the sound of things, Gabe glanced up at the ceiling as he set the coffeepot on the stove to heat up.

There was something about the plain exuberance of that ruckus that set a frozen patch at the back of Gabe's heart to thawing. What Lizbet clearly considered an act of childish rebellion struck him as a blessing. Something he'd longed for, without realizing it.

"Shouldn't I be doing that?" Lizbet asked.

A little startled, though of course he'd known she was there, only a few feet away, Gabe turned to look at Lizbet, one eyebrow raised in silent question.

After a heartbeat or two, he realized what she meant; she thought, since she was officially his cook and housekeeper, that he ought to leave duties like brewing coffee to her.

"No," he said, with quiet directness. "It's the least I can do, after that cold ride from town."

She shivered, as if at the memory of the near-freezing winds they'd run into, and nodded her head as if conceding a point.

Then she looked up at the ceiling—the noise had not abated—and stated, "I'll go upstairs and tell them to quiet down."

"Let them be," Gabe said quietly, though it wasn't his place to tell this woman how to raise her charges. "They're full of energy, and this is a way of letting some of it out. And that includes Hector."

At the mention of the dog's name, Lizbet's tight shoulders eased noticeably. "What if they break something?"

"This is a farmhouse, Miss Fontaine. Not a mansion. Anything that gets broken can be replaced—or done without." This wasn't entirely true, as it happened, since Gabe still kept some of Bonnie's porcelain figurines and other delicate treasures in the bedroom they'd shared, and he would have been devastated to lose them.

There was little chance of that, because he'd locked that particular door before driving into town to meet with John and collect the newcomers to the household from Ornetta's place.

He had another reason for keeping the room locked as well. Frankie's dollhouse was finished now, and mostly furnished, and the sled he and John had built at the blacksmith shop was there, too.

He didn't want the children—or Lizbet—to see the things he'd made for them until Christmas morning. And that included the hinged jewelry box he'd fashioned for Lizbet.

Maybe it wasn't a suitable gift for a man to give his housekeeper, but that was of no great concern to him at the moment. He wanted to give Lizbet something she would enjoy.

"Still," Lizbet said, picking up the conversational thread and then hesitating as though torn between rounding up the marauding children and remaining in the kitchen within the radius of the cookstove, "I don't want you thinking I'm going to allow those two to behave like reckless scoundrels." When their eyes met, Gabe saw real worry in hers. "I need this job, Mr. Whitfield."

Yet again, Gabe longed to lift Lizbet to her feet and pull her into his arms, hold her tight against him, stroke her beautiful hair and murmur words of comfort and reassurance into her ear.

All of that. And more.

Heat was surging through the water in the enamel pot, and Gabe took care reaching for the tin of ground coffee beans on the counter nearby and measuring in a few heaps.

He liked his coffee strong, and so did John.

He hoped Lizbet did, too. Pity he hadn't thought to ask first.

Before Gabe could find the right words to assure Lizbet he wasn't about to withdraw his offer of a job on account of two noisy children, the back door swung open and John Avery stomped in, grinning widely as he removed his hat and coat and kicked off his boots.

There were holes in his socks, Gabe noted, oddly grateful for the mundane distraction. The man needed a wife, that much was sure.

John wasn't above darning his own socks, any more

than Gabe was, but his friend packed so much hard work into his days, between running the blacksmith shop and laboring over his sermons, that he was too tired to do much of anything when he was done.

"Is that coffee about ready?" the big man boomed, nodding at Lizbet. "I'm sure ready for some."

"Almost," Gabe said, amused. And grateful to have such a friend as John Avery. During the darkest days of Gabe's life, the steadfast warmth of that preacher blacksmith's friendship had been like a ray of pure light falling into Gabe's dungeon of sorrow. "Just waiting for the grounds to settle."

"Good," John said. Overhead, Hector and the kids were still playing loudly. He smiled again, his attention on Gabe. "Must be nice, hearing a fine noise like that after such a long time."

Gabe felt a jab of sadness, remembering when his own little Abigail had chased Hector—or been chased *by* him—all over the house and yard.

As if John knew what Gabe was feeling, he sighed quietly, then pulled back a chair at the table.

"May I?" he said to Lizbet, all courtly, like a man who lived in a castle instead of a narrow closet of a room off Ornetta Parkin's upstairs hallway.

Was it wrong, Gabe wondered, that his moment of grief was pushed aside in that instant by a distinct flash of plain old ordinary jealousy?

Yes, it was wrong, and Gabe shook it off, busied himself pouring coffee into three clean mugs. He didn't have any claim on Lizbet Fontaine's affections, he reminded himself sternly, in the privacy of his own mind.

In any case, John was in love with his childhood sweetheart, Mabel Dunsworthy, and soon she'd be traveling out to Montana to stay for good. She and John would be married, right and proper.

The clatter upstairs subsided presently, and Frankie and Jubal and Hector arrived back in the kitchen in a cluster.

Gabe's heart lifted at the sight of them.

"Where are we going to sleep?" Jubal demanded. "We looked in all the rooms, except the one that's locked, and there are beds in all of them, so we can't make out which ones are for us."

"There are *a lot* of rooms in this house," Frankie put in.

"Which one is Hector's?" Jubal asked innocently. "I want to sleep in *his* room."

John laughed.

Lizbet tried to hide a grin.

And Gabe, seated at the table with the two adults by then, smiled a genuine smile. He was glad he had, too, though it had hurt the muscles around his mouth a little, stretching them in ways they weren't used to being stretched.

"I reckon that would be the one on the front right-hand corner of the house," Gabe replied, after some thought, which was mostly pretense, because mentally, he had already assigned them rooms, Lizbet included. "You can see the barn and the cottonwood trees lining the driveway from there."

Jubal punched the air and crowed with delight.

"You don't want to share a room with your sister?" Lizbet asked the boy, looking mildly surprised. "I thought you didn't like sleeping alone."

"I won't be alone, silly," Jubal informed her, jubilant. *"Hector will be with me!"*

EIGHTEEN

That night, after a tour of the house and a good supper, which Lizbet prepared herself with meat from the smokehouse, potatoes from the root cellar and fresh eggs from Gabe's hens, she cleaned up the kitchen while he and the children went outside to bid John Avery farewell.

John had stayed for the meal, and though he had said nothing untoward, there had been a light lingering in his kindly eyes throughout, especially when he glanced at either Gabe or Lizbet.

He was happy for his friend, happy for her, and that knowledge filled her with quiet joy. Sure, Gabe could have done without a housekeeper, she'd known that from the first, but *John* would have known how lonely his friend had been. And, because he'd lived under the same roof with her and the children at Ornetta's place, and because Lizbet had confided some of her concerns in him, John also knew how badly she had needed work and a place to live for the children as well as herself.

Lizbet sighed, looked around the kitchen in case any task had been left undone and decided to go upstairs to her new room and unpack some of her things. Her spring and summer frocks could remain in their trunks until they were needed.

The room was large and situated at the back of the house, next to Gabe's.

Knowing this, and feeling foolish all the while, she had nonetheless checked for adjoining doors and found none. She trusted Gabe—wouldn't have accepted a live-in housekeeping position from him if she hadn't. Still, it paid to be cautious.

And how well did she really know the man, after all?

There were four windows overlooking the pasture and, in the near distance, a series of small hills, thick with trees. Although the cottonwoods had long since dropped their lovely, shimmering leaves, there were tall pines and blue spruce and Douglas fir.

Above them, on this quiet night, hovered a milky, transparent moon.

Lizbet smiled, remembering how Gabe had pointed out those trees to the children upon their arrival and told them it would soon be time to hike up one of those hills and chop down a Christmas tree.

He had a certain blue spruce in mind, too. Had kept his eye on it for a while now.

She let her mind drift back to the moment he'd raised the subject over breakfast.

"It's a particularly fine tree," he'd said. "Tall and full, and it smells like heaven."

"What does heaven smell like?" Jubal had asked, prompting a smile from Gabe.

Frankie had elbowed her younger brother lightly and said in a lofty tone, "He means the tree smells good, silly. The part about heaven was just a figure of speech."

"Can we go soon?" Jubal had cried, probably wondering what a "figure of speech" might be.

Gabe had nodded Lizbet's way. "Whenever your big sister says it's all right," he'd replied.

After shifting her thoughts back to the present, though, Lizbet's smile faded. Christmas was barreling down on her like a boulder just loosed from a mountainside.

She had almost no money, and she had not wanted to ask Gabe when she would start to receive wages. She needed nothing for herself, at least not at present, but it made her ache to think she wouldn't be able to purchase more than a handful of penny candy for the children.

That would be their Christmas.

Tears threatened, but Lizbet blinked them back. She was tired, that was all. She always got teary when she needed to rest.

Be grateful, Elizabeth Fontaine! she lectured herself silently, and with spirit. *You have a place to live and work, and the children are safe. Let that be enough.*

Wearily, she sighed and began putting her stockings and nightgowns and underthings away in the drawers of the pinewood chest set against the wall opposite the windows.

As she continued this task, it occurred to her that, while

there was an indoor commode downstairs, there was no bathtub and no hot and cold running water in this house, like there had been at Ornetta's.

How would she bathe, with so little privacy?

Another self-lecture came to mind. *Stop looking for problems. You're bound to find plenty of them if you don't change the direction of your thoughts.*

She paused in her unpacking and listened for Gabe and the children. Were they still outside in this cold? Surely John had gone back to town by now.

Lizbet began to fret.

What was Gabe thinking of, keeping them out there for so long?

She was about to go downstairs, put on her coat, boots and gloves, and investigate when she heard a happy yip from Hector, laughter from Frankie and Jubal, the low rumble of Gabe's speech, and a voice she didn't recognize.

Soon the children and the dog were upstairs, and the men *downstairs* were arguing.

Had William found them? Or had Henry Middlebrook come to castigate her as a loose woman, living in shameless disregard of Christian precepts?

Lizbet's blood froze at the possibilities, but immediately thawed as good sense returned.

Whoever this man was, he was young.

And he was determined to hold his own.

Frankie and Jubal and Hector all burst into the quiet sanctity of Lizbet's room, squeezing through the doorway in a cluster.

"There's gonna be a fight!" Jubal cried, as if delighted.

"There's another Mr. Whitfield here now," Frankie added, clearly troubled. "How are we supposed to speak to *one* Mr. Whitfield without the *other* Mr. Whitfield thinking we're speaking to *him*?"

"I wouldn't worry about that right now," Lizbet told her small brother and sister, though she was worried herself.

What if Jubal was right? It would not do if a physical altercation broke out inside this house. There were children here, for heaven's sake.

As the voices belowstairs rose, Lizbet's consternation increased. No doubt, this other Mr. Whitfield was Gabe's younger brother, Finn. The one he'd told her about, on the way out of town.

Why did he sound so angry?

Wasn't he glad to see his brother again?

"Stay here," Lizbet told the children, shaking the dreaded finger of warning in their small, bewildered faces. "And know, both of you, that if you disobey me, you will go to bed directly after you get home from school every single day for a solid week!"

They both shrank back in surprise.

Gabe would be driving them to school every morning,

as weather permitted, and then going back to fetch them in the afternoons. Which begged the distracted question of whether or not their presence—and her own—were more hindrance than help.

Two minutes later, she had stormed down the stairs and across the parlor to thrust open the door to the kitchen.

"*Don't you dare come to blows in this house!*" she heard herself shout. And despite the accompanying chagrin, she did not retreat or lower her voice. "There are *children* right upstairs!"

Both Gabe and the other man turned to stare at her, evidently shocked to silence.

Lizbet was already losing her steam; ordinarily, she did not give in to fits of temper. "Honestly!" she added, with conviction.

Gabe's anger faded almost instantly from his face and countenance, though he didn't move. The other man, handsome with light brown hair and clever hazel-colored eyes, grinned at her and then *bowed*.

Lizbet, so vociferous only moments before, was stricken silent.

"I'm Finn Whitfield," the young man said, "and you shouldn't believe a word my brother has said about me." Then, after straightening, he put out a hand to her. "And you are most certainly the woman who has poor Henry Middlebrook on the verge of a stroke."

The mention of Mr. Middlebrook took Lizbet further

aback and renewed Gabe's anger. He turned Finn to face him by wrenching hard at his left arm and then gripped him by his snow-dappled lapels and shook him hard.

"*Enough,*" he hissed into his younger brother's implacable face. "Don't say that man's name under my roof!"

Finn shrugged free of his brother's grip, although Lizbet knew he only managed it because Gabe had loosened his fingers.

"Easy now, Big Brother," he nearly crooned, although he was looking at Lizbet. Assessing her with a look of polite appreciation. "I was just running off at the mouth. I'm not here to criticize your immoral behavior."

Gabe grabbed hold of him again, this time by the front of his sodden shirt, up close to the throat. "Miss Fontaine is my housekeeper," he growled, never looking away from Finn's now-solemn face. "Nothing more. You can say whatever you want about me, but *you will not* imply that there's anything immoral going on here. Do you understand me?"

Finn said nothing, and his cheerful attitude had vanished.

In fact, Lizbet felt sorry for him.

"*Do you understand me?*" Gabe repeated, in a raspy voice.

Lizbet, fearing he meant to choke an answer out of this brother of his, decided to step in.

"Gabe," she said, forgetting all about her determination to address him only as Mr. Whitfield. "Calm down, please. We all need to calm down. The situation has clearly gotten out of hand."

Gabe released Finn with such force that the fellow almost lost his footing. If the kitchen table hadn't been there to collide with, he surely would have landed on the floor, backside first.

Lizbet was beginning to wonder if she ought to be concerned about Gabe's temper. Suppose he became angry with her, or with one or both of the children? Would he raise his hands to them?

Perhaps his gentle manner had been a facade all along, calculated to lure her to Whitfield farm. Did he mistreat the animals, whip the horses or punish poor Hector with violence when the critter misbehaved?

Of course not. She was getting carried away, that was all.

With that thought, reason returned to her tired mind, and she watched Finn sink into a chair and gaze up at his brother with an expression of plaintive fatigue.

Gabe subsided, breathing hard. He was not a violent man.

"Are you going to make me sleep in the barn?" Finn asked his older brother, with new mirth in his changeable eyes. Obviously, he knew the answer.

"You can sleep in the parlor on the sofa," Gabe allowed, still endeavoring visibly to regain his self-control. "Jubal's sleeping in your old room now, and I won't ask him to leave it."

Finn shrugged. "Fair enough," he said. "I'm half starved, though. I've been out of work for a while, and my funds are running low. I'm back to try my hand at being a farmer—if my brother will give me the chance."

Gabe said something in response to that, something not especially polite, but Lizbet didn't register his words for a few moments.

When she did, she closed her eyes and gripped the back of a chair to steady herself and stiffen her suddenly wobbly knees.

You're here because you and Henry and that partner of his want to mine this land for silver, not because you've finally decided to take on your share of the responsibility for keeping this farm going.

Lizbet nearly wept, because she knew instinctively that the partner Finn had mentioned was her stepfather.

It was happening. William was coming back.

She knew it.

With or without Marietta, William was coming back because he and Henry Middlebrook had reached yet another evil accord and worse, Finn, whom she was inclined to like, was in cahoots with them.

And now she might lose the children, once and for all.

NINETEEN

༃

Gabe forgot Finn existed when he saw Lizbet grip the back of one of the kitchen chairs, shut her eyes and turn deathly pale.

Immediately, he rounded the corner of the table and gripped her firmly by her upper arms, then lowered her gently onto the chair she'd been grasping so tightly that her knuckles were bone white.

She was trembling.

"Lizbet!" Gabe gasped. And from then on, although neither of them would ever be able to pinpoint the moment things changed, she was no longer Miss Fontaine to him, and he was no longer Mr. Whitfield to her. "Lizbet, what's wrong? Are you ill?"

She shook her head, her eyes still clenched shut, and her lowered lashes were suddenly wet with tears.

Finn, for once making himself useful, pumped cold water into a cup and brought it to the table.

Gabe carefully pried Lizbet's fingers loose from each other and eased the cup into her hands, keeping it steady until she finally took hold herself.

She opened her eyes, took a sip, looked up into Gabe's

face and whispered, "It's William that Henry Middlebrook is expecting," she said, in a near whisper. "It's William."

Gabe crouched in front of her. "Your stepfather?"

She managed a nod and, yet again, Gabe ached to take her into his arms and hold her.

"Henry did mention the name William," Finn admitted awkwardly, standing somewhere at the periphery of Gabe's vision. "I didn't think—"

"You never do," Gabe answered, his voice clipped. But all his concern was focused on Lizbet.

"Take more water," he urged her, still crouching in front of her chair.

After two or three cautious sips, she set the cup on the table, but she was still trembling. "Dear God," she murmured, as one in a daze. "He's going to take Frankie and Jubal away." Her green eyes were wild now, frantic. "What am I going to do, Gabe? *What am I going to do?*"

Gabe took her cold hands in his and held them firmly, though he was careful not to squeeze too hard. "Don't you think you might be getting a little ahead of yourself, here?" he asked quietly. Then, after a glance toward the door to the parlor to assure himself that Frankie and Jubal weren't standing there, listening in, he went on to say, "William isn't going to take the children, Lizbet. He abandoned them, remember? He's coming to Silver Hills for another reason entirely—because he thinks he can throw in with Henry and get rich mining this farm." Here, he paused, shot an angry glance in Finn's direction. "And that, I assure you, isn't going to happen, either."

Finn wilted a little, but he didn't have an answer ready.

Lizbet shook her head again, despairing. She was so white with distress that Gabe let go of her hands and held her face instead, feeling the softness of her skin against his work-roughened paws. "No," she said brokenly, "William *doesn't* want the children—and that's the worst part, don't you see? He'll take them to punish *me*, not because he's turned into a devoted father. He'll do it because I thwarted his plan to marry me off to that awful man!"

"Shhh," Gabe said, and, without thinking, he kissed her forehead. "Don't borrow trouble. I'll ride over to Painted Pony Creek first thing in the morning and have a word with Judge Bates. He's a good man, Lizbet, and the fact that Keller left his children the way he did, while *you* continued to care for them will carry weight with him."

"Maybe you ought to stay here, Gabe," Finn interceded, his tone speculative now.

"I'm not really interested in your opinion just now," Gabe informed him, rising to his feet to face his brother.

Finn spread his hands out from his sides and looked truly contrite. "Middlebrook made me an offer, that's all. I didn't agree to go after the mineral rights to this land— you didn't give me a chance to explain that when I got here."

Gabe was at once relieved that his kid brother was alive

and well and ready to throttle him for throwing in with a pair like Middlebrook and Keller. "Make up your mind, Finn. Are you still a Whitfield, or are you just a lackey, pandering to those two in hopes of filling your own pockets?"

Tears glistened in Finn's eyes. "I admit I considered their offer, but I knew right away that I wasn't going to accept it. I know how you feel about this land, how Dad and Granddad and Great-Grandad felt about it. I came back because this is home, and because you're my brother." He paused, swallowed visibly, then went on. "You've got to believe me, Gabe. I'm on your side."

Gabe felt a strong stir of hope for this prodigal brother of his, and he relaxed his guard a little. He knew Finn well, despite their long separation, and he was telling the truth.

"Half this farm is still yours," he said. "And I guess I couldn't stop you if you decided to dig for silver on land you own. Just know that if you do that, Finn, you'll be dead to me."

Finn looked pained. "Gabe, we could be rich."

"I don't give a damn about being rich. I care about this land, and everything the family went through to hold on to it through hard times."

"Fair enough," Finn said, with a sigh and a slight lift of one corner of his mouth, an attempt, Gabe supposed, at a grin. "I give you my word, Gabe. There will be no mining on Whitfield property unless you agree."

"I won't," Gabe said flatly.

"I'll get my satchel," he told Gabe, his tone lighter than before. "I left it on the step in case you flung me back out into the storm."

Gabe gave a sigh of his own and rose to his feet. "Get your stuff," he told his brother. "After I'm sure Lizbet is all right, I'll rustle up some dry clothes for you. With luck, you won't come down with pneumonia before morning."

"I'll put it off as long as I can," Finn replied, with pert amusement. "The pneumonia, I mean. Wouldn't want to be any trouble to you, Big Brother. After all, you've got this sacred farm to maintain, and you don't need any distractions."

"Just go," Gabe said, weary but reassured. "And if you want food, help yourself. The pantry is full."

Finn slid a sympathetic, respectful glance Lizbet's way. "Look after the lady," he said. "I'll be fine."

Lizbet was slowly regaining her composure, and when Gabe had reheated the coffee and poured her a cup to steady her nerves, she made an attempt at a joke. "It looks as though John was right," she said, after a sip and a quick pulling in of her cheeks. "Your coffee has to be chewed."

After that, she seemed to regain her strength, moment by moment.

"And I'm not afraid of William Keller *or* Henry Middlebrook," she said, straightening her spine as she spoke. By then, Finn had retrieved his bag from the back step and retreated to the parlor.

"I think I'd better look in on Frankie and Jubal," Lizbet went on, when Gabe didn't speak, pushing back her chair to rise, though he promptly prevented that by resting on hand lightly on her shoulder.

"Sit awhile," he said. "I've got to go upstairs to get some bedding and the like for Finn anyhow. I'll see how the kids are doing and report back to you—how's that?"

Lizbet favored him with a rather flimsy smile that, nonetheless, made him feel as if he might drift upward, untethered by gravity, and bang his head on the ceiling.

"They can be a handful," she warned, but she looked relieved to stay behind. Probably wanted more time to collect herself.

Finn was in the parlor, seated in one of the armchairs and pulling off his boots. As a boy, his demeanor had usually been one of impish good humor, and it heartened Gabe to see the brother he recognized.

"You can't go off and leave that woman alone, Gabe," he said. "Not to ride over to Painted Pony Creek for a lawyer or anything else. She needs protection, and you know it."

"From you?" Gabe retorted lightly, without slowing his pace. He'd reached the foot of the staircase when he heard Finn's answer.

"Henry Middlebrook is a dangerous man," he said. "I remember that from the old days. When somebody gets in his way, he's likely to do just about anything. Knows he's already hell bound, so why not get his revenge any way he can?"

Gabe paused, gripping the newel post with one hand. "If you haven't told me everything you know about what he and Keller are planning, you'd better say so right now."

"He didn't tell me anything. It was his housekeeper, Ruth, who filled me in—I got to town yesterday, and Middlebrook invited me to stay the night at his place. I was almost broke, so I agreed, rather than spend my last dollar on a hotel room or ride out here so you could raise hell with me for mentioning silver mines first thing.

"That woman is bitter as hell, for reasons of her own, which I am too much the gentleman to reveal. What I *can* tell you is that Henry and William met years ago, back in St. Louis. Henry loaned William a boatload of money a while back, and William promised him a young, pretty wife in return, in addition to repayment. Now, having failed to meet the conditions of their original agreement, William's gone and reneged on the rest of the deal, too, because the lovely Lady Lizbet wouldn't cooperate, and now poor old Henry is mad enough to pull up railroad spikes with his teeth."

"What made Middlebrook agree to a plan like that in the first place?" Gabe asked. "He's not the type to buy a pig in a poke, so to speak. And there's no call to point out the awkward inference, because we both know Lizbet is a beautiful woman. What I'm saying is, Henry never laid eyes on her until last fall, when she stepped down from the jitney."

"Indeed, Lizbet *is* beautiful," Finn replied, spreading his hands for emphasis. "And it just so happens that you're wrong, for once in your life. The old man knew that firsthand, because he saw her at a big party of some sort back in St. Louis, according to Ruth. He's been obsessed with her ever since."

"Does Lizbet know that?" Gabe was actually thinking aloud, not querying his brother. "That Henry set his sights on her way back then? Because it seemed to me, he was a stranger to her when she arrived last September."

"I have no idea," Finn admitted, rising from his chair and moving to the sofa, where he began pushing at the cushions with both hands, probably to determine if they would be comfortable to sleep on. "Why don't you ask her?"

Gabe said no more but simply went on upstairs.

The first thing he did was check on the children, as he'd promised Lizbet he would.

Jubal and Hector were sprawled on the bed in Finn's old room, side by side. Hector was awake, but the boy lay spread-eagle on top of the covers, face down and still wearing his shoes.

"Hey, buddy," Gabe said, in a near whisper, his heart swelling a little. "Let's get you tucked in for the night."

Jubal stirred slightly as Gabe removed his shoes and maneuvered him under the covers, but he didn't wake up.

Frankie, it turned out, was better situated.

She lay in the bed Gabe had moved into the space that had once been Bonnie's sewing room, a lantern burning on the bedside table, a book propped up on her little chest.

Again, Gabe's heart was affected.

"Is everything all right?" she asked tentatively, when she saw Gabe in the doorway.

By *everything*, Gabe knew, she meant Lizbet. And to this child, Lizbet probably *was* everything—or very nearly so.

Was William Keller greedy enough, coldhearted enough, to separate Frankie and her brother from the person they loved most?

Possibly, he was, and that raised Gabe's hackles again, tired though he was. His argument with his brother—which had begun maybe five seconds after Finn stepped over the threshold and immediately lobbied him to sell the mineral rights, if not the farm itself—had taken a lot out of him.

"Things have calmed down considerably," he answered mildly, chagrined that he and Finn had frightened this child and probably her brother, too, by shouting at each other the way they had. "Your big sister is fine, but I reckon it's safe to say she thinks you ought to be sound asleep by now."

"You won't tell her I lit the lamp, will you?" Frankie asked, worried. "She'd be mad, because we're supposed to let her do that, always. Because there could be a fire."

Gabe was making no promises. "Just don't do it again, Missy," he said. "Fire is nothing to play around with." It wasn't very dark upstairs, because the moon was almost full and the curtains were open. She'd lit the lamp because she wanted to read, and the moonlight, bright as it was, wasn't enough.

He hesitated on the threshold, unsure whether he ought to walk over and put out the thing himself or keep a proper distance. He wanted Frankie and her brother to feel safe in this house.

Frankie solved the problem by stretching out one arm and turning the key at the base of the glowing lamp, thus quenching the flame.

"Good night, Mr. Whitfield," she said.

"Good night, Frankie."

He was turning to leave when she spoke again, her voice soft and tentative and heartbreakingly young. "Mr. Whitfield?"

"What is it?"

"Please don't let my father make Lizbet get married to that awful Mr. Middlebrook," she said. "She might do it, if it means keeping me and Jubal."

Gabe hesitated, still on the threshold, his back to Lizbet's innocent little sister, searching both his mind and his soul for the right response.

Finally, he said, "I mean to make sure that doesn't happen, Frankie. No matter what it takes."

TWENTY

෴

Wasting no time, William arrived first thing the next morning, a passenger in Henry Middlebrook's automobile, both of them jammed into the front seat and so bundled up against the persistent cold that only their begoggled eyes were visible.

Their arrival was not unexpected, of course, and any element of surprise was rendered moot by the racket that contraption made, its engine popping and roaring and grinding as it traveled over a road so frozen that the children thought they'd be able to skate on it, if they had skates.

Gabe, Finn and Lizbet were all outside waiting, in their warmest clothes when the automobile finally stopped a few yards away, and the engine chortled and boomed its way into silence.

Before Lizbet could say a word, Gabe stepped forward and said authoritatively, "Mr. Keller, you're welcome to come inside. Henry, you can wait in the barn while we talk. Finn will keep you company. He has a few things to say to you anyhow."

Henry's eyes blazed with such accusing fire that Lizbet privately wondered if his anger wouldn't be enough to keep him warm, all those layers of clothing notwithstanding. "I have not come to take away your paramour, Whitfield," he very nearly spat, once he'd unwound the heavy scarf covering his mouth and pushed his goggles up onto his forehead. "Lizbet Fontaine, you are a fallen woman. A flagrant sinner. You needn't think for one moment that I would stoop to marry such a one as you!"

Lizbet was secretly relieved, of course, though she knew Henry could still make her life difficult, and probably would for as long as he lived. He'd been furious when she'd dared to confront him, and he would keep the ugly gossip running, every bit as noisy and poisonous as the exhaust from his automobile.

"Well, now, Henry," Gabe said, in a near drawl, "you're a fine one to call anybody else a sinner." He turned, caught his brother's eye. "Finn, see our cantankerous visitor to the barn, won't you?"

Finn shrugged affably and then nodded. "Come along, Mr. Middlebrook," he said, as cheerfully as if he were about to lead the man on a tour of some majestic museum. "It's surely warmer in the barn than it is out here."

Throughout this entire exchange, William had been sitting in rigid silence, his head down, his eyes still covered by his goggles, which looked as though they'd frosted over.

To Lizbet, he resembled a prisoner, not a free man.

When he finally removed the goggles, he fixed his plainly miserable gaze on Lizbet. There was a pleading element in his stare, rather than the anger she had been bracing for since the night before, when Finn had told them of his imminent arrival, and she was puzzled by that.

Curiously, instead of fear, Lizbet felt an emotion more closely related to pity.

What, she wondered, had William come to say?

He didn't look as though he had the strength to make demands upon her. Slowly, as though injured and wary of making his condition worse, William climbed down from his seat and made his way carefully toward Lizbet and Gabe, who were waiting on the back step, just off the kitchen.

Henry, blustering and disgruntled, had allowed himself to be squired in the direction of the barn, with Finn half pushing, half pulling him along, chattering cheerfully away the whole time.

Lizbet, Gabe and William were all in the kitchen, where a brisk fire was crackling away in the belly of the cookstove, before she got a clear look at her former stepfather's face.

He was gaunt, his skin pale, his eyes rimmed in dark circles.

Lizbet felt a rush of compassion for this man her mother had apparently loved. This man who, for better or worse, was the father of Frankie and Jubal, whom she cherished.

Without William, they would never have existed.

It was a sobering thought; Lizbet could not imagine a world without her little brother and sister in it.

"Sit down, William," she said, "before you faint dead away."

"Are the children here?" William asked. These were the first words he had spoken. Henry, now exploring the Whitfield barn with Finn, had done all the talking.

Lizbet glanced at Gabe, who was leaning against the long work counter, arms folded, expression watchful but otherwise benign. She wondered briefly if Gabe, too, had taken note of William's shrunken spirit. Then she answered, "They're here. They're safe and well and, William, they're *happy*."

A painful smile flickered across William's lips, there and then gone, as quickly as that. He groped for a chair, making an awkward attempt to pull it back and failing to catch hold.

Gabe moved to pull the chair out for him, saying nothing.

William collapsed onto the seat, folded his arms on the tabletop and rested his face on them.

Lizbet noted the bald spot on the crown of his head and was surprised she'd never noticed it before.

Not that it mattered.

"She's left me," William said, his voice muffled by the sleeve of his coat, which looked, like its owner, somewhat the worse for wear. "Marietta has left me, Lizbet."

Lizbet and Gabe exchanged glances, then Lizbet sat down next to her late mother's onetime husband and cautiously rested a hand on his shoulder. It was trembling, as though his very soul were weeping within him. And for all her great dislike for this man *and* for his second wife, tears sprang to Lizbet's eyes.

She would never have wished such sorrow on anyone, not even Henry Middlebrook, hateful old miscreant that he was.

"I'm sorry to hear that," she said very quietly.

Gabe, who seemed to believe that coffee was the remedy for every ailment, whether of body or spirit, went to the stove, pot holder in hand, and picked up the pot.

"I'm destroyed," William went on.

"Nonsense," Lizbet said, having suddenly recovered her spunk. "The world is full of marriageable women, William. You'll meet someone else in time."

"The world is *not* full of women like Marietta," William bemoaned, as Gabe set a strong cup of coffee in front of him and took up his post by the counter again.

Proof that God is real if I've ever heard it, Lizbet thought.

Women like Marietta *were* rare enough, and it was so by the grace of the good Lord, in Lizbet's opinion.

"William," Lizbet said firmly, as he finally raised his head from his arms and gazed at her bleakly, "sit up straight and behave like a man. Why are you here?"

Her bluntness seemed to rally William a little, a very little, which, Lizbet supposed, was half a step in the right direction.

"Why, to say goodbye," William replied, blinking, with an expression that might have been surprise. "To you and to—to the children."

Something within Lizbet soared, though she managed to stay seated and control her desire to leap to her feet and shout *glory hallelujah!*

"You're leaving them with me?" she asked, instead, and her voice was cautious and quiet, part jubilation and part stunned disbelief.

"Yes," William said, "if you'll take them."

"Of course I will," Lizbet said, mildly impatient now. "But it has to be forever this time, William. You can't dangle them over my head ever again. You'll have to write out a document verifying that I'm their legal guardian and sign it. Before witnesses."

"I'll do that," William said, sounding defeated.

Silently, Gabe left the room, returning a few minutes later with writing paper, a pen and a bottle of black ink.

William spent nearly half an hour drafting and redrafting the document, but in the end, his decision was clear. Frankie and Jubal were Lizbet's legal charges and would remain so until they reached adulthood.

"Shall I call them downstairs now, William?" Lizbet asked, clutching the papers to her bosom the moment the ink had dried, as though they were holy writ, just discovered. "So you can speak to them yourself?"

But William shook his head. Bumbled to his feet and began to wrap himself in mufflers before putting on his coat.

"I've decided against dragging this out with some big display of emotion. Besides, I've never been a father to them, really, so there's no point in putting them through a scene. They won't miss me on any account." He paused, then reached into the pocket of his coat with one shaky hand. "I wrote them letters, one each. You can read them to the children at your discretion—whether that's directly after I leave today, or years from now, when you deem them ready."

Lizbet took the two damp envelopes William extended and laid them aside. Belatedly, and none too steady on her feet, she stood.

"Where will you go now?" she asked the weak, broken man standing before her. "What will you do?"

"I'm headed back to St. Louis. I have friends there. I'll lick my wounds for a while, and then—" Here, William paused, attempted a smile and emitted a heavy sigh instead. "And then I suppose I will try to get back on my feet."

Lizbet merely nodded.

Gabe, who hadn't spoken in a long while, ventured a question of his own. "Why did you come out here with Henry Middlebrook?" he asked. "You could have come alone."

"He insisted," William replied, "and I needed a ride. If you'd given him the chance—let him into the house—he'd have done some gloating. Being booted to the barn first thing must have really thrown a monkey wrench into his works."

"What does he have to gloat over?" Again, it was Gabe who spoke. Lizbet, for her part, suddenly felt breathless, like a foot racer collapsing just across the finish line.

William, already moving toward the door, gave a sputtering, hollow laugh, devoid of all humor. "About his forthcoming marriage—to Marietta. As soon as she and I are officially divorced—and believe me, the decree is already in progress—they will become husband and wife. In the meantime, Henry will be financing her first film. Come spring, the lights and cameras will arrive in Silver Hills, and a moving picture will be made." He stopped, spread his hands for emphasis. "She'll be a star. Who could compete with that?"

Lizbet found herself sympathizing with William again, though a part of her still wanted to slap him silly just for being the way he was.

The man had a worm for a spine.

As for Marietta and Henry? Well, they definitely deserved each other.

And the people of Silver Hills would be delighted to have an actual moving picture filmed in their very own town.

For Lizbet, the worst was over.

She could be happy now. Move forward with confidence.

A look passed between Lizbet and Gabe.

She had no clue what he might be thinking, but beneath all Lizbet's joyous relief, something else was stirring. Something beautiful and dangerous, something mysterious.

The revelation struck her with a wallop.

That something was *love*—pure and simple and powerful.

Love for Gabe Whitfield.

Gabe Whitfield, who could not give his heart to any woman, because he'd buried it with his wife and daughter.

TWENTY-ONE

☙

Frankie and Jubal had witnessed their father and his salty and still-bristling companion driving away from Jubal's bedroom window, Lizbet discovered, when she went upstairs, for they were still standing there, looking small and confused and very, very vulnerable.

"We heard what Father said," Frankie announced, when Lizbet entered the room. It was airy and spacious, that room, and Hector rested comfortably in the middle of Jubal's unmade bed. "He left us letters, and we get to stay with you for good, and Marietta is going to be in a real moving picture."

Lizbet nodded solemnly. It was the strangest sensation, drifting between two very different and very strong emotions—relief that Frankie and Jubal would not be going away and sorrow for these children. Even though they'd wanted to stay with Lizbet all along, they had to be wounded by their father's disinterest in them, too.

She didn't know whether to weep or to laugh with joy. "Does it bother you," she began gently, "that he didn't say goodbye to you?"

"I'm *glad* he didn't try to say goodbye," Jubal replied,

with defiant emphasis. "If he did, I would have kicked him in the knee!"

With that, Jubal burst into tears, rubbed at his eyes with the backs of both hands as if to push them back. "I *hate* him!" he cried, just as Lizbet reached him.

Dropping to her knees, she practically crushed the little boy, she hugged him so hard. Then, with her free hand, she reached out to squeeze Frankie's hand.

Murmuring reassuring sounds, rather than clear words, Lizbet rocked Jubal back and forth in her arms as he sobbed.

It was then that Lizbet heard footsteps on the stairs; they were slow ones, and a little uncertain.

Gabe.

By then, Frankie was crying too, albeit softly, rather than furiously, as her brother did, and Lizbet drew her into the embrace, holding both children close and letting them cry.

Lizbet knew Gabe had paused in the doorway of Jubal's room, and she wondered what he was thinking.

If she'd been him, she thought distractedly, she would have been wondering why men like William could turn their backs on their own children while men like him, Gabe, *lost* their much-loved, much-wanted little ones.

Life could be so cruel, so unjust.

"They've gone," Gabe said, when Jubal and Frankie had calmed down somewhat and Lizbet got back on her feet. A long pause followed Gabe's words, then he went on, "I was wondering—well, maybe now isn't the time—"

"Gabe," Lizbet said, hastily drying her cheeks with the hem of the apron—one of many—that had belonged to Bonnie Whitfield. "*What* are you trying to say?"

"Well, I guess I was about to say that this might be a good time to go out and get that Christmas tree we talked about. Before the weather takes another bad turn, I mean."

It had always amazed Lizbet how resilient children really were, and the next moment reinforced her belief.

Jubal let out a startling whoop of joy, passed Lizbet like a circus performer fired from a cannon and leaped into Gabe's arms.

He caught the child deftly and held on. For a long and touching moment, Gabe's eyes were closed. Was he remembering his little girl, and how it had been to hold her like he was holding Jubal now, in a strong, protective way?

The thought—and the sight—so moved Lizbet that her eyes filled again, and her throat constricted.

In that moment, she dreamed of having children of her own, plump, sweet babies—fathered by this man.

This man who could never love her.

Gabe opened his eyes, met her gaze and then silently held out a hand to Frankie.

The girl hesitated, then she went to him, too, though not in the same rushed way her brother had. Instead, she stood shyly at Gabe's side, his arm around her shoulders now, and leaned against his side.

It was all Lizbet could do not to emulate the children by rushing to Gabe herself.

Of course, she refrained.

Gabe was a kind man. He knew Frankie and Jubal had suffered a major emotional blow, and he wanted to help them.

But he wasn't looking for a new wife and family, Lizbet reminded herself, as she had moments before.

However fatherly Gabe might have seemed just then, he was most likely missing Bonnie, and little Abigail. Acutely.

After all, it should have been Bonnie cooking his meals and cleaning his house—not that she, Lizbet, had done much of that, having only arrived the day before—and it should have been Abigail going out with him to find a Christmas tree. The child would have been six now, from what John had told her, bright and beautiful as a sunflower in spring.

Lizbet, who had good reason to be happy and thankful, felt a hollow space open up in her heart.

"Can we, Lizbet?" Jubal cried, his little face red and swollen, his eyes bright with contrasting excitement. "Can we please go with Mr. Whitfield to get the Christmas tree?"

"You're welcome to come along," Gabe said quietly, watching Lizbet's face as he set Jubal back on his feet.

She drew a deep breath, wiped her cheeks again, this time with the palms of her hands, and drummed up a smile.

"I'd like that," she said.

It was a long hike to the place where the tree Gabe had chosen stood, lush-limbed and fragrant, but the fresh air and the effort were good for everyone.

Finn came along, as did Hector, and when the children began to tire, he carried Frankie piggyback, while Jubal rode happily on Gabe's shoulders.

The tree *did* seem special, standing there in the snow, rimmed by sunlight and clearly sketched against a blue sky that seemed to go on forever.

"Seems a shame to cut it down," Finn remarked, only a little out of breath from the climb with Frankie on his back.

"We can't *kill* it!" Frankie wailed suddenly, in complete agreement with Finn. "I don't *want* a Christmas tree if we have to kill it!"

Gabe met Lizbet's gaze and winked.

He *winked*, this man so well acquainted with bone-crushing sorrow.

"Reckon I'd better hike back to the barn for a shovel," Finn said, with an exuberance he'd clearly had to drag up from the depths of his being. "Gabe and I will dig this spruce up and haul it home to dry off in the barn. Tomorrow, one of us can saw a barrel in half, make a big plant pot and put the tree in that. That way, after Christmas is over, we can take it outside again and plant it somewhere close to the house."

Lizbet's heart warmed. She knew Gabe and his brother had their private differences, but in that moment, she decided Finn Whitfield was as decent a man as his brother, down deep.

Frankie and Jubal cheered.

Gabe smiled, though somewhat wistfully. "Good idea," he conceded, addressing Finn.

With that, they all hiked back down the hill toward the house and barn. It was an easier journey, since gravity was working in their favor now, but by the time they reached the back door, Frankie and Jubal were nearly asleep on their feet.

Silently, Lizbet thanked God—and Gabe Whitfield—for the healthy distraction from their sadness over William's departure.

She gave them each a cup of stove-warmed apple cider, chosen from among the many glass jars of food items stored in the pantry. Gabe had admitted that he hadn't put up all those things himself; he'd paid a woman down the road to do it.

Having hung their coats over the backs of their chairs, because they would be leaving the house again soon to climb back up that arduous hill and dig up the spruce tree, which was at least eight feet tall, Finn and Gabe sat at the kitchen table and drank reheated coffee.

The children consumed most of their cider, but they were nodding off in their chairs. Lizbet roused them enough to stand up, took both of them by the hand and led them upstairs to their rooms.

Hector, probably tired himself, followed Lizbet and the children, though a little reluctantly. When Lizbet looked back at him over one shoulder, he was hesitating—heading back toward the stairs, then toward her and Frankie and Jubal again.

Lizbet had never had a dog of her own, even as a child, since her mother had already been in fragile health, and the housekeeper, Evelyn, hadn't wanted anything to do with "filthy four-legged critters," as she'd called them. Animals belonged outside, not in.

Now, looking at Hector, she felt a rush of gentle affection, a certain gladness, as if she'd searched and searched for something lost and finally found it.

"You go with Gabe and Finn, if that's what you want to do," Lizbet told the dog, in a whisper, expecting Jubal to protest at any moment.

Hector gazed up at Lizbet as though he'd been taken by surprise, confronted by an angel of light, and when she continued along the corridor, he followed, nails clicking along the hard wooden floor.

While the children napped, Lizbet bustled about the kitchen, opening more jars containing stew meat and various vegetables. She scrubbed and peeled carrots and potatoes from the cellar, washed and sliced onions, ransacked the shelves for spices.

Once the stewpot was chortling away atop the cookstove, she mixed flour and other ingredients and made biscuit dough.

It was nearly dark when Finn and Gabe returned from the hill, dragging the tree behind them, its exposed roots dark against the snow.

Lizbet watched them through the window over the kitchen sink, having wiped away the steam first, and she felt a little leap of excitement within her, thinking how excited the children would be.

Hector must have heard his master approaching the house, because he came bounding into the kitchen on a dead run, like a racehorse on the home stretch.

With a smile, Lizbet opened the back door for the dog, so he could shoot out into the twilight, but put a hand out to stop Jubal from following. He and Frankie had already had supper, as well as separate baths in front of the kitchen stove, and were now in their nightclothes. Despite the naps they'd taken, Lizbet knew they would sleep soundly that night and most likely awaken at the proverbial crack of dawn, ready to "help" Finn and Gabe bring in the tree and place it in front of the parlor windows.

Lizbet had already cleared the spot.

"But I want to see the tree!" Jubal nearly howled, thwarted.

"You'll see it in the morning," Lizbet promised firmly. "It's almost dark now, and it's very cold outside. Be a good boy and help me set the table again. The men will be freezing, and very hungry."

Probably considering himself one of the men, Jubal quieted down and puffed out his chest. "I'll help them put the tree up in the parlor tomorrow," he said. "They'll need me."

"I'm sure they will," Lizbet replied, handing Jubal two clean plates. "Be careful," she added. The dishes were Blue Willow, and they had been Bonnie's. Lizbet would have been mortified if they'd been broken, but, at the same time, the children needed to learn to help out and to treat pretty things gently.

Frankie busied herself fetching silverware and napkins while Lizbet stirred the stew.

She was proud of that stew; it was savory and rich, and it would nourish two tired men, who'd been out in the freezing cold, fetching a Christmas tree down from a hilltop, up to their knees in snow when they were up high, for a good part of the day.

Finn and Gabe didn't come into the house immediately after their return; Lizbet knew, as did the children, that they would tend to the horses and that dear old cow and feed the chickens before they came inside. How those birds survived in such weather was a mystery to Lizbet, who had firmly believed, when she was Frankie's age, that eggs came from the corner market, not the hind end of a feathery, squawking hen.

The back door finally opened, just as Jubal was asking a question that stopped them all in midstep.

"Do you think Mr. Whitfield would ever want a little boy?"

TWENTY-TWO

Do you think Mr. Whitfield would ever want a little boy?

Jubal's question stopped Gabe on the threshold, causing Finn to plow into him from behind, and the emotions that struck him like a runaway train were too complicated to sort out, beyond the strange mingling of hope and—what? Sorrow? Regret?

Lizbet was standing across the room, and when their gazes met, Gabe saw sympathy in her eyes, and what might have been a silent apology.

"Supper's ready," she said aloud. "Come in, both of you, and get warm."

Come in—get warm . . .

There was something singularly comforting about those words, probably because he hadn't heard them in so long, not in his own house, anyhow. Ornetta had often greeted him that way when he had cause to stop by her place, but that was different.

This greeting felt, well—intimate—though Lizbet probably hadn't intended that.

Gabe stepped aside so Finn could enter, fumbled with the buttons on his heavy work coat, then remembered to take his gloves off. But he didn't speak.

He was too busy taking in the steamy, welcoming atmosphere of the kitchen, the aroma of venison stew and biscuits just about ready to come out of the oven, the scent of hot coffee, freshly brewed.

It was all such a change from the way he'd been living before, alone, except for Hector, that for a moment or so, he was almost overpowered by the change.

Here, in the kitchen of a house that had been so cold and so hollow for so long, were two hopeful children, faces flushed with anticipation. They'd been there since yesterday, of course, but seeing them now, watching him with wide, eager eyes, seemed new somehow, and definitely profound.

Finn broke the loaded silence with a light elbow jab to Gabe's rib cage. "Come to your senses," the younger man chided. "And get out of my way. If you don't want to eat the delicious meal this lady has so kindly prepared, *I do.*" He gave Lizbet a mischievous wink.

Gabe resented that wink, and he knew why, though he wouldn't have admitted as much to anyone. It was hard enough to admit to *himself*, but he felt strangely territorial where Lizbet was concerned, which was crazy, because whatever the gossips were saying, he had no claim on her, be it sinful or pure as morning dew.

"There's warm water to wash up in," Lizbet spouted, and then looked mildly embarrassed, as though she'd said something ridiculous instead of perfectly practical.

Gabe was still silent as he hung up his coat and hat and moved toward the sink, where the promised warm water awaited, along with towels and a bar of the strong soap required to get a farmer's hands clean after a day of work.

He was still a little off-balance as the boy's words echoed not only in his head, but in his heart.

Did he want a son? Another daughter?

Yes, he did, and no, he didn't, God help him.

Frankie and Jubal were precious children, bright and precocious and unique, each in their own right. Any man would be proud to claim them—any man, that is, besides William Keller, their actual father—and Gabe included himself in that number, even though it landed what felt like the kick of a mule to his midsection.

And that kick was guilt, he knew that.

Guilt because he wanted more children, all of a sudden, not just Frankie and Jubal, but others as well. And that felt like a betrayal of his sweet little Abigail—and of her mother, too.

He and Bonnie had planned on a large family.

So Gabe bumbled and fumbled his way through the rest of the evening, consuming several helpings of stew and half a dozen hot, buttered biscuits, saying little.

Finn, as was his way, took up the slack.

He was full of questions for the children—What did they think St. Nicholas would bring them when he made his rounds on Christmas Eve? Were they planning to hang up their stockings, the way he and Gabe used to do, when they were small? Would they help him bring the baubles and ornaments down from the attic and decorate that very fine tree?

Gabe listened and felt his heart opening more and more, as he was finally able to hope Finn would stay this time. Find himself a wife, build himself a house, a project he, Gabe, would gladly help with.

He thought of the dollhouse for Frankie, hidden in his room, along with the sturdy sled he and John had made for Jubal, Gabe fashioning the base from richly scented pine, John shaping the sleek iron runners that would make the toy *fly* down hills.

He thought, too, of the delicate jewelry box he had been putting together as a gift for Lizbet, and wondered if he should give it to her after all. He was proud of it, and he'd crafted it carefully, but suppose she construed it as a romantic gesture of some sort?

Maybe it would be best to leave the jewelry box where it was, not quite finished, out in the barn, needing only hinges and a catch. He'd already varnished it to a high shine.

Gabe wasn't ready to make any kind of statement, as fond of Lizbet as he was—and, yes, as attracted to her as he was—and with good reason. He knew Lizbet felt *something* for him, and he didn't want to raise false hopes.

That would be both dishonest and cruel.

And so, when the meal had ended and Lizbet had insisted

on clearing away the after-supper mess and then herded two protesting little ones upstairs to read them a chapter of *Tom Sawyer* before bed, Gabe lingered at the kitchen table with Finn, who was watching him with a kind of amused curiosity—and mild accusation.

"What's the matter with you, Gabe?" he asked forthrightly. "That woman must have spent hours spit-shining the place and making the best supper I've had in years, and you hardly said a word to her."

"I'm tired, that's all," Gabe said. It was the truth, but it wasn't the *whole* truth, and Finn clearly knew that.

Finn. There was another puzzle. For a while, he'd seemed to be a rascal and a waster, born to wander, but it seemed he'd changed. Or maybe he'd simply grown up.

In any case, he was good to the children, good to Lizbet. What had happened since the last time Gabe had seen him, almost five years before, that had turned him around?

Had he really given up the mining idea? Or was he simply biding his time?

"You're wondering what I'm up to," Finn said, briefly narrowing his eyes.

They hadn't talked about their argument, that first night.

"You've had dealings with Henry Middlebrook—you even stayed at least one night in his house. And you must have wanted to sell him the right to strip these hills and fields and pastures bare, looking for silver at one point. How do I know you've really changed your mind?"

Finn sighed, spread his hands. "I guess it looks pretty bad," he admitted. "But the fact is, I'm not so different from you as you think I am. I'd like to find a woman like Lizbet, for one thing, and marry her while the marrying was good."

Knowing he shouldn't, Gabe got up from his chair without answering, went to the stove and refilled his coffee mug. At this rate, he wouldn't close his eyes before the sun came up, let alone get the good night's sleep he sorely needed.

Digging up that tree had been a two-man job, and Gabe had sweated through his woolen shirt, even though the weather had been frigid. His entire body throbbed with an ache he knew only a scalding hot bath would ease, and how was he going to manage that, with two children and a respectable woman in the house?

Tomorrow, he reflected, would be just as difficult.

They'd have to cut a barrel in half to hold the tree and fill it with enough dirt to keep it upright, and they would have to dig down to that dirt through the snow, then hack at the ground with picks until they had enough soil to fill the improvised pot. Once they'd trimmed the roots of the tree, being breath-holdingly careful not to cut away too much, they'd have to hoist the spruce into the half barrel and pack cold dirt in around it, enough to make it keep the thing alive *and* steady.

And that was the easy part of the job.

Lugging the whole works through the house and then

on into the parlor was a job for a mule team, not a pair of ordinary men.

"Were you listening to what I just said?" Finn finally demanded, as Gabe returned to the table with his coffee and his heavy thoughts.

"Yeah," Gabe answered rather brusquely. "You said your association with Middlebrook must look pretty bad. That's an understatement, brother."

"I just wanted to get a rise out of you, and I did," Finn said, and there was a note of chagrin in his voice. "You're my brother, Gabe, the only kin I've got left, and I want things to be the way they were before."

"What way was that?" Gabe asked, sounding less interested in the reply than he really was. Pain in the hind end that Finn had been at times, Gabe had missed him.

Missed laughing with him, talking with him. Missed the impromptu horse races over country roads, even the hard work of maintaining a farm, easier because it was shared.

So, it would seem, he, Gabe, already knew the answer to his own question.

"For all that people look up to you for your strength and your kind ways, Gabe, you can be one hard-assed son of a gun. You make up your mind about somebody or *something* and there's no changing it."

Gabe look a measured sip of his coffee, mostly to stall. Behind his facade, he was enjoying the exchange.

In fact, he welcomed it.

Welcomed Finn.

Besides, Finn was at least partly right about him. He had a will of iron, and when he made a decision, it was hard to undo, even though it had been his own.

Even Bonnie, who had loved him with her entire being, had sometimes found him hard to understand—or to reason with.

He wasn't especially proud of the quality, but it had served him well in many ways, and he was fairly certain he wouldn't have lived through losing Bonnie and Abigail without it.

No, he had never considered taking his own life, but only because he knew he couldn't do such a thing to the people who cared about him, like John Avery and Ornetta.

Hell, he couldn't have done that to Hector.

So his own strength had held him upright through the hardest part of his life so far. Without it, he might simply crumble and stop living, die of weariness and sorrow, all without putting a gun to his head or looping a noose around his neck.

"Sometimes," Finn ventured mildly, and it was almost as if he could read Gabe's mind as his words unfolded, one into the next, "a man just needs to let himself fall apart. Yell and weep and shake his fist at the sky. Tell God just exactly what he thinks of Him."

Something inside Gabe yearned to do all that, and more, but there it was, in the way—his own need to steel himself, to maintain control.

He was afraid, he realized—*afraid*—scared to love again, scared to trust the fates, scared to risk more pain, no matter how great the reward in question.

And that, of course, was nothing but plain old cowardice.

Shamed by this realization, Gabe took refuge in skepticism. "You sound as though you speak from experience," he allowed, though his delivery was almost mocking.

"Maybe I do," Finn said, very quietly.

That statement came out of left field, and it undermined Gabe's certainty of his own convictions about who and what his brother was.

The feeling was not a good one.

"How so?" he asked, with an easiness he didn't feel.

Finn sighed, linked his fingers together, bent his head for what appeared to be a long period of reflection. When he looked up, the usual mischievous glint in his eyes had turned to sadness.

"You know why I didn't come home when Bonnie and Abigail died?" he asked, and there were tears gleaming in his eyes. "Because I took sick, Gabe. Came down with tuberculosis and spent better than two years of my life in a sanatorium, waiting for my lungs to heal."

Gabe leaned back in his chair, as though he'd been slapped, hard. "Why didn't you tell me?"

Finn answered without hesitation, and grimly. "You were already furious with me for not sticking around to help out. And not so long after that, you were so torn up about what happened to Bonnie and Abigail, you didn't need another load to carry."

Gabe felt his temper rise a little. "Damn it, Finn, I'm your *brother*. I would have come and fetched you, so you could recover at home."

Finn shrugged his shoulders, a weary gesture. Like Gabe, he was physically exhausted, and almost spent in other ways, too. "That's exactly what I wanted to avoid," he said. "Anyway, all that's behind us now," he replied. "But I will say this, Big Brother—you're a damn fool if you don't open your eyes to what's right in front of you—a woman who loves you and two children who need a father."

Alas, another man might have been drawn toward the promise of a new life, a fresh start.

The fear was upon him in a moment, crushing him beneath its darkness and its weight.

Instead of stepping into the light, as he knew he should, Gabe Whitfield withdrew into the deepest part of himself, and slowly, methodically began rebuilding the defenses Finn had so nearly breached.

TWENTY-THREE

⁓

The morning of December 24 dawned bright and crisply cold, with clear, frost-hardened roads, and when Finn and Gabe came inside for breakfast, after tending to the chores, they had a merry, secretive air about them, as though they'd been conspiring out there in the barn.

Frankie and Jubal were fairly jumping up and down with excitement, even though Lizbet had taken pains to explain to them that St. Nicholas had had a difficult time of late, just as they had, and might not leave the piles of presents they'd received in other years.

They had nodded solemnly in response to Lizbet's words, and they'd both said they didn't care if St. Nicholas passed them by this year, because they got to stay with her and live on Whitfield farm with Gabe and Finn and Hector.

Touched, Lizbet had marveled to see young children demonstrate such mature understanding. She suspected that Frankie no longer believed in the jolly old elf anyway, but she chose to pretend for her brother's sake. And Jubal appeared to be content with things as they were.

For all that, for all the luscious fragrance of fresh spruce permeating the entire house, Lizbet felt downhearted whenever she thought of Christmas morning, when there would be nothing under that splendid tree in front of the parlor windows.

In daylight, it sparkled with tinsel, glass icicles and dozens of tiny stars, carefully cut from the lids of tin cans, according to Finn. He and Gabe had made them together, when they were boys, as a gift to their mother. She, and later Bonnie, had added crocheted angels and embroidered ornaments fashioned from scraps of fabric.

Now here it was, the morning of Christmas Eve, and all Lizbet had in the way of gifts were three fruitcakes—she'd sent Finn to town for the dried bits of cherry and orange and three pounds of walnuts—and he'd either paid for the items himself or charged them to Gabe's account at the general store in Silver Hills. He'd never asked Lizbet for a penny.

She'd wrapped two of the cakes in dish towels fashioned from flour sacks, which Bonnie had apparently saved, and tied them with bows made from quilt scraps, also left by Gabe's late wife and, before that, his mother.

Today, while the roads were still passable, they would all travel into town in the horse-drawn sleigh Gabe had recently purchased—along with a functioning milk cow and another flock of chickens—from a neighbor, an old man who was moving, now that his health was in decline, to Missoula to live with his daughter and her husband.

One of Lizbet's fruitcakes was a gift for Ornetta; the

other, for John Avery. The third would remain in the pantry, to be served when the time seemed right.

Since Gabe had recently paid Lizbet in advance for a month's work, to her great surprise, she had spending money, but life experience had taught her caution.

A person never knew when the rug would be pulled right out from under their feet.

Finn made sure the ride into town was a cheerful experience by singing Christmas carols the whole way, at the very top of his lungs.

Frankie and Jubal sang along, just as loudly, when they knew the lyrics. When they didn't, they made them up.

Gabe was taciturn, as usual, and he was still behaving like a man with a secret, but he made a few good-humored comments on his brother's singing voice, which, if Lizbet would have been forced to say, had she been asked, was no threat to the great opera singers she'd heard at concerts back in St. Louis.

Something was different between the two brothers, too; the hostility was gone.

Their first stop was at Ornetta's boarding house, where Frankie and Jubal would be staying for an hour or two, while the grown-ups tended to business at the general store across the street.

A tall, thick-limbed Christmas tree stood in Ornetta's front window, bedecked with ornaments, some splendid and some tattered, and there were wrapped gifts beneath it.

Ornetta accepted Lizbet's fruitcake and good wishes—Finn and Gabe had secured the horses and crossed the street—very graciously. She seemed pleased with the offering and thanked Lizbet with a kiss on the cheek and a sparkle in her eyes.

"The second cake is for John," Lizbet said shyly. "He must be at his forge, since it's so early in the day."

Ornetta beamed, just as pleased with John's gift as her own. "No," she said, "he's over at the church, practicing his message for tomorrow morning."

Frankie and Jubal, delighted to be visiting the place where they had been so welcome before, shimmied out of their coats, took off their hats and mufflers and mittens and commenced to admiring Ornetta's Christmas tree.

"You go on, now," Ornetta urged Lizbet in a whisper. "I'd love a visit, but there will be time for that later. I know you have things to do."

Lizbet gave her dear friend a grateful hug, instructed the children to behave themselves and hurried out of the boarding house, across the wide and surprisingly busy street and into the woodstove warmth of the mercantile.

The store was decorated for the holiday, with bells and wreaths and even a small crèche displayed alongside a tiny countertop Christmas tree.

The aroma of fresh pine boughs was festive indeed.

Keeping an eye out for Finn and for Gabe, since she planned to give them each a pair of woolen gloves as a

Christmas gift and didn't want them to see what she was buying, Lizbet went about her shopping. Maybe gloves weren't a very thrilling choice, but it was the best she could reasonably do.

Once she'd selected the gloves, she placed them in the hand-carried basket provided, and headed for the section where the toys had been set out. They looked picked over, since it was almost Christmas, but she found a copy of *Heidi* for Frankie and a picture book for Jubal. She added crayons, a packet of coloring paper and two large sticks of peppermint, and that was where her budget ended.

Although she eyed the pretty dolls and the shining red fire wagons and other toys, she did not give in to temptation to buy what she couldn't afford.

Yes, she was employed now, and her and the children's living expenses were mostly covered, but she wanted to save as much money as she could over the coming months.

Since it seemed unlikely that Gabe would ever risk falling in love again, she needed an alternative plan. If she had enough saved, come spring, she and Frankie and Jubal could move back to St. Louis and settle down for good. She'd already written the head of the girl's school where she'd taught since getting her teaching certificate, inquiring about a future position. The letter was in her pocket, and she would send it off when she paid for today's modest purchases.

Did she want to leave Silver Hills and Gabe and Ornetta and John and, yes, even Finn, though his energy often wore her out, to start over from scratch?

No. In fact, the thought of leaving very nearly broke her heart.

But she couldn't wait forever for Gabe to open *his* heart. She was nearly twenty-three years old, already a spinster by anyone's reckoning, and she wanted a *chance* at a happy marriage and at least one child she'd borne herself.

She knew it was impractical of her, but all her instincts said, "Stay."

Could she trust them?

She knew she would never love another man the way she did Gabe, and she didn't want to be an old maid. She could still offer companionship, couldn't she?

Surely some decent, upstanding man would want her to be his wife and the mother of his children.

She was thinking these thoughts when Finn approached, holding an armload of parcels wrapped in brown paper. He grinned and nudged her lightly.

"Penny for your thoughts," he said.

"You wouldn't want them," Lizbet replied, squaring her shoulders. "Complete waste of money."

"Surely not," Finn replied smoothly.

Such charm, wasted. Lizbet laughed and shooed him away—Finn would have stood with her at the cash register if she hadn't.

Once she'd paid for everything and dispatched her

letter, closing her eyes and giving a silent prayer as the storekeeper dropped it into a bag of outgoing mail, she collected her single lumpy package and joined Finn by the door leading to the street.

"Where's Gabe?" she asked.

"He's busy at the moment," Finn answered. "I'm supposed to squire you to the dining room at the Statehood Hotel. He'll finish up here, pick up Frankie and Jubal from Ornetta's and meet us there for lunch."

The meal, served by former fellow boarder, Nellie Carlyle, was hot, aromatic and delicious—roast beef, gravy, boiled potatoes and green beans boiled with bacon. Gabe said very little throughout, but he made a point of sitting next to Lizbet at the table, and that made her heart flutter.

Once they'd all finished eating and Gabe had settled the bill, leaving a generous tip as well, much to Nelly's appreciation, it was time to go back to the farm.

Jubal, who'd received a bag of shining red, blue and silver marbles from Ornetta earlier, clutched them, even though he practically fell asleep at the table.

After helping the boy into his coat and other things, Gabe whisked Jubal up into his arms and carried him out to the sleigh, which was waiting in front of the hotel. Frankie walked primly alongside Lizbet, a miniature lady, showing her the package of colorful paper dolls Ornetta had given her.

Not for the first time, Lizbet imagined the four of

them, Gabe, Frankie, Jubal and herself, as a family, and had to blink back tears.

When everyone was settled and covered in blankets, Gabe snapped the reins lightly onto Shadrach's and Abednego's backs, and the journey home began.

Back at the farm, Gabe dropped Lizbet and the children off near the kitchen door—fat, feathery flakes of snow were beginning to drift down and twilight was already deepening the shadows up in the hills—and then he and Finn went on to the barn.

Supper was light that evening, due to their sumptuous midday repast at the Statehood Hotel.

Lizbet served canned peaches with cream, both of which Gabe had purchased that day at the general store, and the children spent a couple of happy hours playing with the gifts Ornetta had given them.

Frankie seemed fascinated by the paper dolls, with their flapper's haircuts, saucy poses and short skirts, while Jubal pestered both Gabe and Finn into more than one game of marbles.

Once the children were in bed, Lizbet wrapped their gifts in quilt scraps salvaged from a trunk in the attic and placed them under the tree, which was shadowy by then, though a flash of lantern light caught some of the more sparkly ornaments, like the tin stars, now and then.

The effect was so simple, but it was magical, too.

Lizbet said good-night to both Finn and Gabe, who

were playing a cutthroat game of checkers by then and showed no signs of being sleepy, and retired to her room.

She performed her ablutions and went to bed.

Sleep claimed her immediately, though she woke up once, near dawn, thinking she'd heard the merry jingle of sleigh bells.

Silly idea, she'd reflected. *You were dreaming.*

When morning arrived, she was awakened not by the bright winter sunshine streaming in through her window but by Frankie and Jubal, who jumped onto her bed and bounced until she was awake.

She yawned and stretched, briefly forgetting that it was Christmas morning.

The children each grasped her by the hand and literally dragged her out of bed, giggling and hopping from foot to foot.

"St. Nicholas was here!" Jubal shouted, in pure glee. Hector, who had accompanied the pair into Lizbet's room, began to bark, as if to bear witness to the boy's claim. "*He didn't forget us*, Lizbet!"

Confused, Lizbet grabbed her dressing gown—it was modest and warm and covered her as well as any dress would have done—and tried to hush the children.

Finn and Gabe had been up late the night before, playing checkers. It would not do to rouse them so early.

But they were up, with coffee made. In addition, they had done the morning chores, and they were waiting in the parlor when Frankie and Jubal fairly dragged Lizbet down the stairs.

She froze in her tracks when she saw the Christmas tree.

There were a number of packages underneath, but it was the wonderful doll-sized house and the beautiful wooden sled with its sleek runners that the children were so excited about.

Frankie rushed to the dollhouse and knelt beside it, almost reverently, trying to hug the whole thing, though it was nearly as tall as she was, then standing up. "It's mine!" she cried. "Mr. Whitfield said so!"

Jubal, meanwhile, had perched on top of the sled, while Hector circled curiously, sniffing as he went. "And this is mine!" the little boy crowed. Then, in a more subdued tone, he added manfully, "But I mean to share it with Frankie. It's big enough we can ride it together."

Lizbet was literally unable to speak, and when her gaze found Gabe's, she nearly wept with gratitude.

She mouthed the words, "Thank you."

He merely nodded.

While Finn distracted the children with other gifts—Lizbet's and other things, too, a toy car for Jubal and a lovely storybook doll for Frankie, to name only a few—she simply stood there on the stairs, too amazed to move.

"Come and sit down," Gabe said, speaking at last, walking over to the base of the stairs and extending a hand to her.

Lizbet was suddenly and painfully aware that she was still in her nightclothes, which was improper, whether they covered her well or not, but Gabe caught hold of her hand before she could flee.

His smile was gentle, and it shone in his eyes, though that sadness he carried was still there, too.

He led her to the parlor sofa, which still held Finn's bedding, and sat her down.

Then he brought her a box wrapped in silver paper and tied with red ribbon, *real* ribbon, shining and smooth.

"Open it," he said, very quietly, and for a moment, it was as though they were the only people in the room.

With trembling hands, Lizbet obliged. Inside was a beautiful wooden jewelry box with roses carved into the lid and a velvet lining.

"Ornetta put in the velvet," Gabe explained, looking shy.

"But you built this," Lizbet marveled. "With your own hands."

"Yes," he said, very quietly.

"Oh, Gabe," she whispered, stroking the top of the box with the fingers of her right hand and thinking of the humble gift she'd bought for him. Woolen gloves, for heaven's sake. "It's lovely. Thank you."

"You're most welcome," he said.

They simply gazed at each other for the longest time, and Lizbet was almost certain he would have kissed her, if Finn and the children hadn't been present.

It was Lizbet who broke the spell—if she hadn't, she would have initiated a kiss herself—by rising to her feet, clasping the jewelry box close and announcing, "I'll just get dressed now, and then I'll start making breakfast."

She was jubilant, at least on the inside, and once she came back downstairs, the pots and pans made a merry sound as she set them on top of the stove.

TWENTY-FOUR

⚘

That Christmas day was to be a memorable one, for many reasons, but primarily because of what happened at its very end, when all of them—Gabe, Finn, Lizbet and the children had opened gifts, eaten breakfast and proceeded to church, all in a happy bunch of woolens and laughter and more of Finn's awful singing.

There, they'd heard John's sermon and sung hymns of the season and greeted everyone who had made their way to the gathering, despite the gray clouds clustering on the southern horizon.

For the first time since the passing of his wife and daughter, more than three years before, Gabe had not chosen to sit in his usual out-of-the-way place; he sat beside Lizbet, clean-shaven, hair neatly combed, wearing his best clothes.

If there was whispering or pointing of fingers, neither Gabe nor Lizbet took notice.

Lizbet concluded, for her part, that the serious dressing down John Avery had given his congregation previously had shamed the judgmental ones into silence.

Or perhaps they had simply stayed home, too scandalized to attend a church that was clearly careening off into the dark abyss of unforgivable sin.

It was telling, Lizbet had reflected more than once, how little resemblance these people bore to the One whose birth they had gathered to celebrate.

After church, it was back to the Statehood Hotel, John accompanying them this time, for a wonderful meal of turkey and all the traditional trimmings.

Twilight was almost upon the town of Silver Hills and its surroundings, of course, when none other than Henry Middlebrook approached the table.

He looked ominous, and there was a glint of bitter triumph in his tiny eyes. Fortunately, the dining room was packed, and the children were across the room by then, chatting with some of their schoolmates.

Before Middlebrook could speak, both Finn and Gabe were on their feet, with John following suit, and it was clear from the way the three men held themselves that they had not risen out of respect, but because they were prepared to put up a strong defense.

"I see you sat together in church today," Middlebrook said, in an ugly, insinuating tone. "I'm surprised there wasn't a protest." His hard gaze flickered to John for a moment, then touched on Lizbet, and she squirmed under it. "I might even call it a miracle."

"You were there," Gabe said evenly, and there was

something in his voice Lizbet had never heard before. Something not to be trifled with. "Seems to me, the real miracle here is that the roof didn't fall on your head."

Middlebrook gave a mocking little huff of a chuckle and let his gaze rest on Lizbet again. "He'll never love you, you know," he said, and she was afraid it was true. "He's a dead man, for all practical intents and purpose. Might as well have been buried with his wife and child."

Gabe started forward, but John stopped him, gripping his arm with a hand that routinely forged molten iron into horseshoes and sled runners and wheels and axles.

"Henry," John said, in his ponderous, preacher's voice, "get out of here and leave these people alone. Your behavior is reprehensible, and don't think the Lord won't take note of it, because He will."

Henry bowed his head slightly at John's words, but he still looked pleased with himself as he turned and walked away. After all, he was soon to be married to Marietta, and the producer of an actual moving picture. He had plenty to be smug about.

It was only after he had gone that Lizbet realized the whole place had gone silent. John's voice had certainly been heard, throughout most, if not all, of the dining room.

And she was mortified, feeling all those eyes upon her. Upon everyone at their table.

Furthermore, as terrible as Henry's words had been, the

ones about Gabe never loving her, they were most likely true.

As if in reassurance, kindly people came forward.

Men patted shoulders and murmured words of friendship to Gabe and Finn and, of course, John.

Women patted Lizbet's arm and the tops of the children's heads and said gentle things.

So, to Lizbet's relief, it appeared that not *everyone* in Silver Hills believed her and Gabe to be blatant sinners on a greased track to hell.

The ride back to the farm was a quiet one, by contrast, and for Lizbet, Christmas was essentially over.

The children, burrowed down in blankets, fell asleep.

Once they reached home—when had she started thinking of the farmhouse as home? It was a *temporary* place of residence—Finn and Gabe each carried a sleeping child into the house.

John, who had come along, riding his horse behind the sleigh, escorted Lizbet inside, where she hung up her coat and gloves and tried to shake off the things Henry Middlebrook had said in the hotel dining room.

She made a great clatter, starting a fresh pot of coffee, knowing Gabe and Finn would do the evening chores and be cold and tired when they came inside.

"He needs you, Lizbet," John said, surprising her so that she nearly dropped the tin of ground coffee beans and the spoon she was using to add them to the pot. "Gabe Whitfield is one of the finest men I've ever known, and that's saying something, because I've been around. My daddy was a tent preacher, and he dragged my mama and me and my brothers—" He paused there, smiled wearily. "Matthew, Mark and Luke, those are their names, if you can believe it—from one side of this great nation to the other. Roaming the countryside like that, a man meets just about every kind of person, and out of all of them, Gabe stands out like a lighthouse on a dark, stormy sea."

Coffee preparation completed, admittedly by rote, Lizbet suddenly lost all the starch in her knees and dropped into a chair.

"Did you know about the dollhouse?" she asked.

John drew up a chair and sat down across from her. "Yes," he said gently, reaching out to give her hand a brief squeeze. "Originally, he was building it for Abigail. When she and Bonnie died, he put it away, unfinished, and I don't believe he went anywhere near it again until he decided Frankie ought to have something nice for a Christmas present. He brought it into the house and refurbished it."

"It's beautiful," Lizbet almost whispered. "But now it's going to remind him of the daughter he lost every time he looks at it."

"What matters here, Lizbet," John replied, "is that he hauled the thing to the house, carried it inside, and worked on it every night for weeks. That's where there's a crack in the wall, and there's light shining through it. Gabe's tired of being miserable. He's ready to break down that wall, but he needs you to be there, literally right there, so he knows he has someone to live for."

"How do I do that?" Lizbet asked fretfully. "Gabe is so *solitary*. He doesn't want anyone to see how badly he's hurting."

"He has to open up," John insisted, though with tenderness for his friend's dilemma. "He's got to realize that he can't get through this alone."

"You're his best friend," Lizbet reasoned. "Couldn't you reach him?"

"I've tried," John said, with a sigh. "If we get too close to the crux of the matter, he withdraws into himself, slams the doors and fastens the window latches. It's you he needs, Lizbet. On some level, past my ability to understand or explain, he's been waiting for you."

"But what do I do?" she reiterated. "How can I help him, John? I've seen that sorrow in his eyes, sensed how far-reaching it is. It really *is* a wall, and I saw him disappear behind it today, after Henry Middlebrook said the things he did."

"Henry's words were harsh, no question about it—it's beyond me why a person would go to church Sunday after Sunday and then turn around and act the way he does. But those very words, awful as they were, have caused another crack in Gabe's defenses, a vital one, and that might be what saves him."

The coffee boiled, and Lizbet let the grounds settle for a few minutes before pouring cups for herself and John.

They were sipping in silence, each thinking their own thoughts, when Finn entered, covered in large flakes of snow.

Lizbet looked past him. "Where's Gabe?"

Finn looked worried. Why hadn't she noticed that until now?

At her question, he glanced briefly at John, then turned his attention back to Lizbet. "Something's happened with Gabe. I'm not sure what it is."

Lizbet froze. "What do you mean, 'something happened'? Is he hurt? Sick?"

Finn looked reluctant, and he'd gone a little pale. "No," he said, which was not enough information to suit Lizbeth.

"Finn Whitfield, tell me what's going on!"

Finn let out a long breath. "Gabe's gone up to the graveyard. I told him he ought to come inside instead, since the weather's about to take another turn and its so dark, with no moon, but he wouldn't listen. It was as if he didn't hear me, in fact."

"I'm going to find him," Lizbet said, untying her apron and heading for the coat hangers beside the back door.

John rose to his feet. "Are you sure, Lizbet? Maybe it would be better if Finn and I went instead?"

"I'm sure," she said, wrapping herself in her coat.

John's face was full of emotions he was unlikely to turn loose. "I'll go with you. Show you the way."

Lizbet nodded her agreement and yanked open the door, letting in a rush of frigid air.

When Finn started to follow, she ordered him to stay with the children.

He didn't argue.

John bundled up quickly. He lit a lantern, since it was dark as dark, any moonlight snuffed out by the thick snowfall, and led the way across the yard, past the barn, and halfway up the hill behind it.

Gabe's boot prints were visible in the snow.

"You can go the rest of the way on your own," John told Lizbet, once they'd stopped, holding the lantern above their heads.

Not as confident as she had been before, Lizbet was wringing her hands. "What should I do, John? What should I say to him?" she nearly pleaded.

She needed an answer.

"Do you love Gabe Whitfield?" John wanted to know.

"Yes," Lizbet said, with a certainty she hadn't known she possessed.

"That's enough," John confirmed. "Just go to him, and when you get there, do what your heart tells you to."

Easy for him to say.

What if Gabe got angry, sent her away, not only from the graveside, but from his house—his life?

She soon came to the conclusion that, at this point, such fussing was selfish. What was happening here was about Gabe, not her, not Frankie and Jubal.

Gabe.

So she trudged on alone, holding the lantern John had handed to her moments before, and when she rounded a little bend in the pathway, there was Gabe. He was kneeling near the grave where Bonnie and Abigail had been laid to rest, his face buried in his bare, cold-chafed hands.

"Gabe?" Lizbet ventured silently, sidestepping her way around to stand where she could face him.

He said nothing, not at first. Perhaps he hadn't heard her or noticed her approach.

She waited. Watched.

And then he spoke, not to her, but to Bonnie and little Abigail. "It's time to let you go," he said, with great sorrow and yet with resolution, too. "Both of you. You made me promise to live, Bonnie—remember? And it's time I kept that promise. There's a woman—Lizbet is her name—and I care for her. I care for her a lot. So I'm saying goodbye."

He began to weep again, albeit silently, and not with the ragged sobs she'd heard from a distance. Still, she could sense the despair rising within him like lava in a volcano, fixing to blow at any moment.

She wasn't afraid, though. Not for herself, at least.

She set the lantern on top of a nearby grave marker, knelt, facing Gabe, feeling the cold and the wet seep through the fabric of both her dress and her coat, turning her knees numb, and not caring about any of that.

The despair finally grew too great and too powerful to be contained, and Gabe gave a cry so primal and so heart-rending that Lizbet thought something had torn his very soul from its moorings and tossed it aside.

Awkwardly, she scooted forward, laid her hands on his shoulders. "It's all right," she said softly, with tears slipping down her cheeks. "It's all right, Gabe."

He made no move to dislodge her hands from his shoulders, but he didn't acknowledge her, either. He just threw back his head and howled once more, in an agony she couldn't begin to imagine, then he howled again.

Lizbet waited until the cries had dissolved into sobs, and she leaned forward, then, and rested her forehead against Gabe's.

She could feel her tears mingling with his, and there was something sacred about that. It was a communion of sorts, though explaining it was and would remain far beyond Lizbet's powers of description.

When Gabe had quieted down enough to speak instead of crying out, he did. His voice was hoarse and ragged.

"I love you, Lizbet," he said. The statement was more confession than vow. "I love you and I need you."

Lizbet cried harder and kissed Gabe on the mouth that had just given her the promise of everything she'd ever hoped for in her life. "And I love you, Gabe Whitfield."

"I'm not ready for a wedding," he told her frankly. "I can't be a husband to you, not yet, but I *want* to, Lizbet, and when I said 'I love you,' I meant it."

"I'll wait," she said.

He was looking into her eyes by then, though they were both half blinded by the ever-thickening snow. "I have some healing to do," he said, "but you have my word, Lizbet. If you'll have me, I'll marry you, come spring."

She cupped his beloved face between her mittened palms. "We'll heal together," she promised. "In the meantime, I think we ought to get back to the house before we both catch our deaths."

Too late, she realized that she'd chosen that last word badly, but before she could change it, Gabe was getting to his feet and bringing her with him.

He looked down at the gravestone, marked with the names of his wife and daughter, but there was something different in his expression now, something glowing behind the ravages of the sorrow he'd just released.

"They're not here," he said, and Lizbet knew he meant that Bonnie and Abigail had long since gone on to an infinitely better place.

"No," Lizbet confirmed, holding his hands in hers. "I never knew Bonnie, of course, or Abigail. But from what

I've learned about them—from John and Ornetta and Finn and you, I think it's safe to say they would want you to live and be happy, Gabe. I think they would want that more than anything."

He gave a brief nod of agreement, but said nothing.

He took Lizbet's chin in his hand, tilted her face upward and kissed her deeply and for a long time.

When the kiss ended, Lizbet almost collapsed from the loss of it.

Gabe, holding her upright with one arm, actually chuckled at her reaction.

Then he reached for the lantern, casting a golden glow into the swirling snow and gloom, and, still holding Lizbet's hand, he led her away from what was gone, toward the endless possibilities of what was yet to come.

Spring was still a way off, and so was the wedding.

But the process of healing had definitely begun, for Gabe and for her as well.

And that was enough.

★ ★ ★ ★ ★